KT-389-759

Scarlet Wilson wrote her first story aged eight and has never stopped. She's worked in the health service for twenty years, having trained as a nurse and a health visitor. Scarlet now works in public health and lives on the West Coast of Scotland with her fiancé and their two sons. Writing medical romances and contemporary romances is a dream come true for her.

Also by Scarlet Wilson

A Touch of Christmas Magic
The Doctor's Baby Secret
One Kiss in Tokyo…
Christmas in the Boss's Castle
A Royal Baby for Christmas
The Doctor and the Princess
The Mysterious Italian Houseguest
A Family Made at Christmas
The Italian Billionaire's New Year Bride
Resisting the Single Dad

Discover more at millsandboon.co.uk.

LOCKED DOWN WITH THE ARMY DOC

SCARLET WILSON

MILLS & BOON

First published in Great Britain 2018
by Mills & Boon, an imprint of HarperCollins*Publishers*
1 London Bridge Street, London, SE1 9GF

Large Print edition 2019

ISBN: 978-0-263-07794-0

MIX
Paper from
responsible sources
FSC® C007454

This book is produced from independently certified
FSC™ paper to ensure responsible forest management. For
more information visit www.harpercollins.co.uk/green.

Printed and bound in Great Britain
by CPI Group (UK) Ltd, Croydon, CR0 4YY

This book is dedicated to all the loyal readers of Medical Romance all over the world.

Thank you for letting me write for you and for enjoying Medical Romance.

CHAPTER ONE

AMBER BERKELEY LEANED against the wall of
the elevator as it descended to the ground floor.
The doors reflected a kind of odd image. She'd
forgotten to check in the mirror before she left.
Her half-up-half-down hair looked like some
kind of bewildered lost animal on her head. She
let out a laugh. She didn't even want to know
what her bright pink lipstick looked like. Truth
was, she didn't really care.

Tonight's ball was bound to be full of special-
ists and consultants who were all too important
to breathe. She loved her job, but some doctors
just seemed like a different breed entirely. Self-
important. Self-interested. Amber didn't waste
much time on people like those.

Tomorrow she was lecturing at one of the most
prestigious conferences in the world. And she
couldn't pretend she wasn't nervous. Hawaii was
a magnificent setting. One hundred per cent

more gorgeous than most of the places she visited. The Disease Prevention Agency tended to send their staff to investigate outbreaks and try and prevent the spread of infectious diseases.

Most of her time was either spent in the main base at Chicago, or on one of many expeditions as part of a team, generally to places with few or poor facilities.

This five-star hotel in Hawaii was like something out of a dream. She'd even been greeted by the traditional colorful leis on check-in. And, corny or not, she'd liked them. The beach outside had perfect golden sand with sumptuous private loungers and straw parasols complete with serving staff. This part of the main island near Kailua Kona was a perfect piece of paradise.

Her first-floor room had a gorgeous view of the Pacific Ocean, which seemed to change color depending on the time of day. So far today it had gone from clear turquoise blue to light green. Shimmering like a tranquil soft blanket stretching to infinity.

As the doors pinged and slid open, the noise and the aromas of the food surrounded her. The room was full of people talking, a sea of dark tuxedos with a smattering of colored dresses in the mix. She threaded her way through, keeping her chin raised as she glanced from side to side. She had to know someone here. But the sea of faces didn't reveal anyone familiar. Amber's nose twitched. She wanted easy company. A chance to share a few drinks, grab a few snacks and get rid of the butterflies in her stomach for tomorrow.

She stared at a sign on the wall. Ah...there were two conferences on in the hotel—not just the one she was attending. It seemed that a world of business and economic experts were here too.

Just before she'd left, the director of the Disease Prevention Agency had called her into his office. She'd only seen the inside of his office walls on two previous occasions. Once, on the day she'd started. And second, on the day she'd received her promotion.

"Dr. Berkeley," he said solemnly. "I wanted to wish you well for tomorrow. There's been a lot of interest in our contribution to the conference. Thank you for presenting the meningitis research for us."

Amber gave a nod and a smile. "I've loved

being part of the meningitis work. I'm honored to present on it."

The director nodded. "And you're confident you can answer any questions?"

Amber held up the list in her hand. "I've spent the last few months eating, breathing and sleeping meningitis. I think I've got it covered."

The director didn't even blink. "Oh, I'm not worried for you." His eyebrows rose as she stood from her chair. "I'm worried for them. Let's hope they're ready for you, Dr. Berkeley."

She'd smiled as she'd left. It seemed that her take-no-crap attitude was getting a reputation of its own. She wasn't embarrassed by it. Not at all. She'd never seen the point in beating around the bush. She'd always talked straight, to patients and to colleagues. Medics could be notoriously sexist. And Amber could be notoriously blunt.

Had it cost her a few jobs? Maybe. Had it earned her a few others? Definitely.

A guy with a paunch belly and gaping shirt approached her, beer sloshing from his glass. "Hello, gorgeous. Where are you going to?"

She didn't miss a beat. "Away from you." She

didn't even glance at the lanyard round his neck. She had no intention of finding out his name.

She'd always vowed never to go out with a fellow medic. Life experience had taught her it wasn't a good idea.

She glanced around the room again. This was probably her worst-case scenario, wall-to-wall fellow medics, with copious amounts of alcohol flowing.

A few seconds later she met another charmer who refused to let her step around him. "We must stop meeting like this." He grinned as his hand closed around her forearm and his eyes ran up and down her body.

She didn't hesitate. She flipped his arm up and twisted it around his back, catching him completely by surprise and thrusting him in the other direction as the woman next to her laughed out loud. "Yes, we must," she said sharply.

The main bar in the center of the room was currently three people deep. Her chances of getting a drink were slipping further and further away.

Her eyes homed in on another bar on the far side of the room and through a set of doors.

It looked much more sedate. She could have a glass of wine, check out the list of bar snacks then head back to her room and enjoy the view.

She threaded her way through the rest of the crowd. There were a few people who obviously knew one another sitting around tables. Even from here she could recognize the medic talk.

Right now she couldn't stomach that. So she headed directly over to the stools at the bar. There was a broad-shouldered guy already sitting there. He looked as if his whiskey was currently sending him into a trance.

Perfect. Too drunk to be a pest.

Or if he wasn't? She could deal with that.

She smiled as she sat down, crossed her legs and leaned her head on one hand. He might be tired but he was handsome. Actually, he was more than handsome. He was good-looking with an edge of ruggedness. His dark hair was a little rumpled and his suit jacket had been flung carelessly onto the bar stool next to him. She couldn't get a look at his eyes as his head was leaning forward toward the glass. But she could see the lean muscle definition beneath his pale blue shirt, the slight tan on his skin and the hint of bristle around his jawline. She smiled and just couldn't help herself. "Well, aren't you just the original party pooper?"

Jack Campbell blinked and blinked again. Nope. It had definitely happened. Or maybe he was just hallucinating. He stared into the bottom of his whiskey glass again and clinked the ice.

The warm spicy aroma emanating from the woman sitting next to him started to surround him, just as she crossed her long legs on the high stool, revealing the daring split in her floor-length black dress.

Even from here, he'd noticed her the second she'd appeared at the entrance to the ballroom. She was taller than most women, but wasn't afraid to use her height, combining her black sheath dress with a pair of heels and piling her dark hair with pink tips on top of her head. He'd watched her survey the room, ignore a few admiring glances, give short retorts to two men who dared to try and approach her and, now, she'd just crossed those exceptionally long legs and given him a clear view of them. Her black heels had ornate straps and crisscrossed up her calves.

At least he thought he'd watched her. Maybe he was dreaming. Truth was, he was so tired the only reason he was still awake was that his body was craving food. Food he seemed to have been waiting an eternity for.

He gave himself a shake. Maybe he needed another whiskey. The first one was putting him in that strange state between fact and fiction. His stomach rumbled loudly, so he lifted his hand to grab some nuts from a bowl on the bar. Quick as lightning, someone gave his hand a light slap.

For a second he was momentarily stunned. Then he shook his head and gave a smile of disbelief as he turned in his chair.

She was staring straight at him with a pair of bright blue eyes. He couldn't help himself. It was as if the fatigue coupled with a dash of whiskey had reduced all his usual politeness and social norms to a scattering of leaves beneath his feet. "Did you really just hit me? For trying to eat a peanut?"

She gave a shrug. "Yeah, sorry about that. Force of habit."

He raised his eyebrows. "You don't look too sorry."

She pulled a face and waved her hand. "Actually, I've just *saved* you."

Now he was amused. "Saved me from what?"

She shook her head and pushed the bowl away. "Probably some kind of horrible death. Best way to catch some kind of disease." She shuddered. She actually *shuddered*. "If I sent those to a lab I could horrify you."

He deliberately leaned over her, ignoring her orange-scented perfume, and plucked a nut from the bowl, holding it between his fingers. "One tiny little nut is going to fell me?"

She arched her eyebrows and blinked. There was black eyeliner flicked on her eyelid, enhanced by her thick extra-long lashes. With those blue eyes she really was a bit of a stunner.

"If I could put that in an evidence bag right now and send it to the lab I would." She shrugged. "But, hey, it's your poison. Your stomach."

"This is how you meet people? You attack them at the bar and steal their food?"

For a second she looked momentarily offended, but then she threw back her head and laughed.

She put her elbow on the bar and rested her head on it. "Actually, my ambition this evening is not to meet anyone—I just wanted to grab a drink, some food and get out of here."

He gave a slow nod. "Ah, great minds think alike, then."

She looked a little more conciliatory. "Maybe. Sorry about the slap. Bar snacks make me testy. It really is an automatic reaction."

He laughed. "How many states have you been arrested in?"

She sighed. "More than you could ever know."

He could see the way her careful eyes were watching him, obviously trying to size him up. He liked her quick answers and smart remarks. He mirrored her position, leaning his head on his hand for a second as a wave of tiredness swept over him.

And then she spoke. "I'm trying to work out if you're drunk or just in a coma. I'm warning you—I'm off duty tonight."

The corners of his lips headed upward. Maybe he was imagining all this? Maybe he was already dreaming? Or maybe the jet lag was making him see things. If this was a hallucination, those words were *so* not what he was expecting. He let out a laugh. "I could actually be a bit of both. Jet lag and drinking—" he held up the whiskey glass "—are probably not the best idea in the world. But do I care right now?" He shook his head as he downed the remains at the bottom of the glass. "Not really."

Now she laughed as the bartender came over and set a coaster in front of her. "Well, the jet lag explains the accent. But not the complete disregard for your fellow man."

The bartender caught her eye. "What can I get you?"

She looked at his glass. "I'll have what Mr. Happy's having."

Jack raised his eyebrows at the bartender. "Better just put both on my tab."

She drummed her fingernails on the bar next to him. "Who said I wanted you to buy my drink?" Her overall presentation was quite glamorous but her nails were short and clean. Curious. Most women these days tended to have glittery painted talons.

"Don't drink it," he said smartly. "I can easily drink both."

She smiled. A genuine, wide smile. The pink tips of her hair matched the bright pink on her lips.

"You are easily the most crabbit man in the room." She gave a wink. "Is that Scottish enough for you? I learned that from a Scottish colleague."

He tried not to smile as he nodded his head and furrowed his brow. "It's a well-used word. My granny might have called a few people crabbit in her time."

She gave a smile. "Yeah, crabbit. I like that. It means you won't be a pest."

"But you will be."

"Ouch," she said as the bartender brought over the drinks.

She lifted the glass to her nose and sniffed. "What is this, anyhow?"

"Guess."

She tilted her head to the side. "Oh…guessing games. I know it's whiskey. I've just no idea what kind. And here was me thinking tonight was going to be totally boring."

He liked her. He was actually beginning to wake up a little. But that still didn't stop him putting his head on the bar for a few seconds. He closed his eyes and murmured, "I'm dreaming of snacks. I've only eaten airline food for the last twenty-eight hours. And you've stolen the peanuts."

She was still sniffing the whiskey but laughed anyway and grabbed a bar menu. "Haven't you ordered?"

He sighed as he lifted his head again. "I think I ordered around ten hours ago. Apparently the kitchen is busy, but—" his fingers made the quote signal in the air "—it'll get here soon."

She set down the whiskey glass and gestured to the bartender. "Actually, can you give me a glass of rosé wine instead, please?" She gave Jack a sideways glance as she pushed the glass toward him. "This is too rich for my tastes."

He was still leaning on his hand. After a few hours in a fugue, his brain was kick-starting again, along with his dormant libido.

"I've never really met anyone like you before," he murmured.

Her eyes narrowed. "Is that a pickup line?"

He laughed. "I'm too tired and too lazy to try and pick you up, right now. But, hey, look me up tomorrow. I'll probably have a whole new lease of life."

"With those circles under your eyes, I doubt you're even going to see tomorrow. I bet you sleep right through."

He shook his head. "Oh, no. I have to see tomorrow. I'm speaking—at the conference." He gestured behind her. "I should probably be in there right now, trying to charm my way around the room and into a new job."

"You're looking for a new job?" She gave a half smile. "What? Been fired from everywhere in Scotland?"

The bartender set down her wine in front of her, along with the biggest burger and plate of fries Jack had seen in forever. He couldn't help it. "Praise be. Food of the gods."

She sipped her wine and he could feel her watching him with interest as he snagged a fry. "I'm warning you. Try and put any of this in an evidence bag and I'll have to wrestle you to the floor."

She pushed up from her bar stool, leaning over to steal one of his fries. "You Scots guys. You think you're tough. You ain't got nothing on a girl from Milwaukee."

She bit into the fry and nodded. "Better than it looks. And, because it came fresh from the kitchen, I won't tell you any horror stories about it. I save them for the bar snacks."

Her stomach growled loudly and he couldn't help but laugh again.

He picked up his knife. "Okay, then, mystery woman. Since you're obviously the least boring person in the room, I'll make a deal and share with you." He waved the knife at her. "But let's be clear. This isn't normal behavior for me. I'm just too tired to fight."

He cut the burger in half and pushed her half toward her. "But no more insults. And—" he looked down at her long legs "—I still think I could take you."

She picked up her half. He liked that. A woman who didn't pussyfoot around her food. "Okay, then. Because I'm starved and can't be bothered to wait for room service, I'll take your offer." She gave him a sideways look. "You haven't even told me your name."

He nodded as he poised the burger at his lips. "Kinda like it that way."

Her eyes sparkled. "Me too."

She waited a second then added, "Are you really here looking for a job?"

He waited until he'd finished chewing. "I'm still officially in employment for the next two weeks. After that?" He held out one hand. "The world is my oyster. I've had a couple of offers. Haven't decided whether to take them up or not."

"Don't you need a paycheck?"

He paused for a second. "Of course I do. But right now, it's more important I take the right job, rather than just the first one that comes along."

She studied him for a few seconds. He could see a whole host of questions spinning around in her brain, but she was far too smart to ask. Instead she grinned as she stole another fry. "Makes you sound old."

"You think?"

"Definitely."

He shook his head. "I'm not old. I'm just… well-worn."

She laughed again as she took another sip of wine. "At what? Thirty? Thirty-five?"

He choked. "Thirty-five?" He patted one of his cheeks. "Wow. I was really conned by that moisturizer. I wonder if it's got a money-back guarantee."

He leaned a little closer. "I'll have you know I have a whole ten days before I reach the grand old age of thirty-five."

He narrowed his gaze as he looked at her again. "But two can play at that game." He gave a slow nod and took his time letting his gaze go up and down her length. "I'm guessing, forty? Forty-six?"

She let out a little shriek. "Forty-six! Oh, no way, buster. You've had it now." She leaned over him again, her soft skin brushing against his as she lifted the whole bowl of fries out of his reach.

"Not the fries!"

She perched the bowl in her lap and nodded solemnly. "Surely you know a woman of my maturity needs to keep her strength up."

He liked her. He liked her a lot. The room opposite was full of anxious glances and too much "my qualifications are better than yours." Too many people wanting to talk about how wonderful they were as loudly as they could.

Jack was here for one reason. To present his research. To let people know he'd found something that had made a huge difference in a wartime setting. The difference between life and death.

That was the privilege of being an army doctor. He got to try things—sometimes out of desperation—that private clinics and hospitals around the world would throw their hands up at in shock.

But, so far, some of the best medical inventions ever had come from the battlefield. Freeze-dried plasma, handheld inhalers for pain relief, a specially designed applicator for ketamine to treat trauma casualties, and his own particular find—a type of wound dressing part clay, part algae that stopped severe bleeding in under twenty seconds. It had already saved over a hundred casualties who would have surely died. If they started using it in trauma bays around the globe, it could potentially save millions.

Ms. Mystery next to him leaned over and put her hand on his arm. "Hey? Everything okay?"

The feel of her warm hand sent pulses up his arm. He blinked. "Yeah, of course."

She gave a gentle smile. "Thought I'd lost you for a second there. Maybe the jet lag is getting to you after all." Her tone had changed a little. It was almost as if she'd just had a look inside his brain for a second and seen what he'd been lost in.

He gave a small sigh and tried to imagine meeting her in any other set of circumstances than these. "If I was any kind of gentleman, I should be trying to charm you and be swirling you around the ballroom floor in there."

She leaned her head on her hand. "But that's what I like. You're not trying to charm me. In fact, I should be insulted, because it seems as if you couldn't care less." She wrinkled her nose. "I did hear that Scots guys could be grumpy."

He straightened up. "Hey, that's the guys from Edinburgh. Not the guys from Glasgow." He tugged at his shirt, trying to make himself look more presentable. "And anyway, I have charmed you. I bought you chips."

She stared down at the bowl. "Chips?"

He shook his head. "You call them fries. We call them chips."

She pointed to a box behind the bar. "Oh, no. Those are the chips."

He smiled and leaned a little closer. "No, no. They're crisps. And I was just being polite earlier, calling them fries. Didn't want to confuse you."

She threw back her head and laughed, revealing the pale skin on her long neck, then shook her head and leaned a little closer. "The more tired you get, the stronger your accent gets. Any more Scottish and I'll need a translator."

His brow furrowed. "Nothing wrong with my accent. You just need to pay attention—concentrate a little more."

"Says the man who is sleepwalking at the bar."

He waved a fry with his fingers. "I'm not sleepwalking—I'm sleep-*eating*. There's a difference."

She leaned over and snagged another fry. They were dwindling faster than should be possible. This woman was smart, confident and full of sass. He liked that. "So, what brings you here?"

She waved her hand nonchalantly. "Yeah, yeah,

I should be in there too. Schmoozing. But the truth is, I'm not much of a schmoozer."

He raised his eyebrows in mock horror. "You don't say?"

"Hey." She smiled. "It's my one and only true failing as an adult."

"You'll admit to one?"

She nodded solemnly. "One, and only one." Then she laughed and shook her head. "But you? I bet I could write a whole list."

Her stomach gave a little grumble and she started, putting one hand on it as a little pink flushed her cheeks. "Oops, I guess I'm hungrier than I thought."

He looked down at the plates. All remnants of the burger were gone and there were only a few fries left in the bowl.

"I could eat the whole thing again." He sighed.

She looked a little sheepish. "Sorry, I just stole half of your dinner." She waved over the bartender. "Can we order the same again, please?"

The bartender leaned closer. "I have to be honest. The kitchen is a little slow this evening and bar food is even slower. Between you and me, the quickest way to get served is to order room service. You'll get it in half the time because they prioritize those orders."

Jack paused for only a few seconds, and then he stood up. He nodded to the bartender. "You know my room number—can you put it through as a room-service order?"

The bartender glanced between them briefly then nodded. "Of course, sir. Any drinks to go with the food?"

Jack leaned on the bar. "Any drinks for you?"

Ms. Mystery looked stunned for the briefest of seconds. Then he saw that sparkle in her eyes again. He wasn't propositioning her—not tonight at least. He was still hungry and she was good company. He had no qualms about inviting her to his room.

"Diet cola," she said quickly as she stood up from her bar stool. There was a hint of a smile on her lips. He hadn't even had to make the invite; he'd just worked on the assumption she would join him. And it seemed she was taking up the challenge.

He turned back to the bartender. "Make that two, thanks."

The bartender disappeared and he crooked his

elbow toward her. "Looks like I'm about to buy you dinner for the second time this evening." He glanced toward the packed ballroom, then paused. "You okay with this?"

Her eyes scanned the ballroom too and she gave the briefest shake of her head. "I have the strangest feeling I might be in safe hands with you, Mr. Grumpy Scot. I think I can take the chance." She laughed. "And to think, I took this position at the bar because you looked like the least trouble in the room."

As they headed toward the elevators, he couldn't resist. "Honey, I'm more trouble than you could ever imagine."

CHAPTER TWO

AMBER GLANCED AROUND the foyer and tugged nervously at her black suit jacket. She rubbed her cheek self-consciously, wondering if the imprint of her Scotsman's shirt button had finally left her skin.

It was embarrassing. One minute they were laughing and joking, legs stretched out on the bed after they'd shared the second burger; next she was blinking groggily, aware of the rise and fall of a muscular chest beneath her head. She'd peeled herself back oh-so-carefully, removing the arm and leg she had draped around his sleeping form.

For a few seconds she lay rigid on the bed next to him, her mouth dry, trying to work out what had happened. But it only took a few seconds to orientate herself. Nothing had happened. Nothing at all. She was still fully dressed—the only items missing were her shoes, which were strewn across the floor alongside her bag. He was minus his jacket and shoes too, but his trousers and shirt were still firmly in place.

She took a few steadying breaths. His room was almost identical to hers, so she slid almost in slow motion from the bed, gathered her things and tiptoed to the door. It was ridiculous. All that had happened was they'd fallen asleep. Now she thought about it, he'd fallen asleep first and she'd been so relaxed and so tired; she'd meant to get up a few minutes later. Instead it seemed she'd snuggled up for the night.

As she closed the door behind her while holding her breath, she wondered if she should be offended. They hadn't even kissed. And he was more than a little hot. Maybe he hadn't been attracted to her?

By the time she'd reached her room she'd started to get mad. Irrational and pointless, but, hey, that was just her. Half an hour later she was showered, hair tied back and looking as pristine as she could. She grabbed some coffee and fruit at the breakfast buffet and sat down at a table for a few moments.

This presentation was important. She was representing her agency to more than five hundred delegates. She could make connections today that could help her career. Not that she had ambitions right now. She loved her job. But the work the Disease Prevention Agency did was international. Having contacts across the world was always helpful. Last night had thrown her off balance a little. And she couldn't afford to be distracted right now. Nerves weren't usually a problem for her but she couldn't pretend her stomach wasn't currently in knots. She stared at the huge breakfast buffet then back to her untouched fruit. Apple. She picked a few pieces of apple out of the bowl with her fork then followed up with a large glug of coffee.

There was a rumble around the room immediately followed by heads turning. It was almost like being in a room of bobbing meerkats. Her eyes flickered out to the horizon. The ocean looked a little darker and there were some black clouds in the far-off distance. There were a few nervous laughs around her. "Maybe it was one of the volcanoes telling us all to behave," said someone close to her.

"I don't know," said one of the women close

by in a tone Amber didn't quite like. "I wonder if it could be something else."

Just then the doors to the main auditorium opened and people started to file inside. Amber glanced at her program. It was over an hour until she had to speak. The conference organizers had already told her the presentation was prepared. All she had to do was stand at the podium and talk. She'd initially planned to wait outside and practice, but her churning stomach told her that probably wouldn't do anything to quell her nerves. Maybe listening to someone else would be enough distraction to keep her calm.

She picked up her things and let herself be carried in with the crowd, taking a seat near the aisle in a row close to the back of the auditorium. Within a few minutes the lights dimmed and a professor from one of the national organizations delivered the introductory speech. "Our first speaker is Jack Campbell, Senior Medical Officer in the Royal Army Medical Corps. Dr. Campbell has just finished his second tour of duty. As many of you will know, some of our most widely used medical products were first introduced on the battlefield—and it looks like we're about to hear about a new revolutionary product that could help save lives across the globe. I give you Dr. Jack Campbell."

There was a round of applause in the room as a man in uniform walked across the stage to the podium. Amber blinked. Then blinked again.

A medic. He was a medic.

As he started to speak, her skin tingled almost as if his familiar accent were dancing across it. Jack. His name was Jack. The man she'd spent the night wrapped around was delivering one of the keynote speeches of the conference.

Every hair on her body stood on end. Nothing had happened last night. Nothing. But…it could have, if they both hadn't fallen asleep.

Her stomach did a flip-flop. She'd spent the last ten years avoiding any close relationships with fellow medics. And now she'd just accidentally spent the night wrapped around one. Hardly her most defining moment.

Why hadn't she asked more questions? The truth was, as soon as she'd realized he was Scottish she'd assumed he must be part of the business and economic conference. The UK had the NHS—a government-run health service. Her brain had automatically told her that it was unlikely the NHS would send a doctor to the other side of the world for a conference. But a private business—they probably sent employees to international conferences on a weekly basis. And she'd just automatically put him into that slot.

She gave a tiny shudder. That was what happened when you made assumptions. She lifted her head and looked at him again, angry with herself.

She'd found him attractive. She'd liked flirting with him. The truth was, more than she'd expected to. And now he was here. Standing right in front of a room full of professionals and addressing the room.

And boy, could he speak. She sat mesmerized along with the rest of the audience as he described his time in Afghanistan and the sometimes limited resources. He showed a new wound dressing he'd developed—a mixture of clay and algae that could stop severe bleeding and form a clot within twenty seconds.

Amber could almost see the ears pricking up in the room and people sitting a little straighter in their seats. Those twenty seconds could be the difference between life and death.

His accent drew the audience in—as did his demeanor. He was a commanding figure, especially in uniform. He spoke with passion about his work, but was also realistic and even a little self-deprecating. All things that had drawn her to him last night. He acknowledged everyone who'd worked alongside him, fellow doctors, surgeons and army medics. He showed pictures of some of the soldiers who had been treated and had their lives saved by this dressing that had been used in the field. Finally he showed cost pricing for the wound dressings along with approximations of lives that could be saved across the world. She could sense the buzz in the air; it was almost infectious.

Then he just stopped.

After a few seconds people started glancing nervously at each other. The presentation had finished and his image was now being shown on the large screen behind him in intimate detail. As she watched she could almost swear she saw a little twitch at his right eye—those brown eyes that had almost seemed to bewitch her last night. She gave herself a shake. Where had that come from?

His eyes seemed to focus and he started talking again. "This product was conceived in a place of war. It was needed. It was essential to save lives—and it will be essential to saving lives in the future. War is never a situation you want to be in. People die. Families are devastated and lives change...forever."

He took a deep breath. "What makes me sad is that we need something like this. I'm sad that, even though we're no longer in a time of war, because of gun and knife crime, this product will continue to be needed."

His words echoed across the room. It was the way he said them, the change in timbre of his voice. She could hear the emotion; she could almost reach out and touch it. Even though the temperature in the room was steady, she could swear that a cool breeze swept over her, prickling the hairs on her arms.

People around her were openmouthed. Then slowly, but surely, applause started throughout the room. Within a few seconds it gathered pace and Amber couldn't help but smile as she glanced at the nods of approval and the conversations starting around her.

"Do you think we should get it?"

"It would be perfect for paramedics."

"What an investment opportunity…"

The professor crossed the stage again, shaking Jack's hand enthusiastically. He then launched into the next introduction. "Our next speaker is a doctor from the Disease Prevention Agency."

Amber felt a wave of panic.

"Amber Berkeley has been working there for the last five years. She specializes in meningitis and will be presenting some of the latest research into emerging strains. Please welcome Dr. Amber Berkeley."

Darn it. She stood up quickly. She'd come in looking for distraction and Jack Campbell had certainly met the criteria. Usually she would spend the five minutes before a presentation going over things in her head and taking some time to do controlled breathing. But she hadn't even thought about the presentation the whole time she'd been in here. Somehow her attention had all been focused on her mystery almost-suitor from last night.

She walked smartly down the auditorium, climbing the steps and shaking the professor's hand. Her heart was thudding so loudly she almost expected everyone else to hear it.

She glanced at Jack, who was giving her an amused look. Rat fink. Could he sense her panic? "Dr. Berkeley," he said with a nod of his head as the corners of his lips turned upward.

"Dr. Campbell," she answered as coolly as she could, trying not to take in how he filled out his army fatigues. She was sure he could have worn his more formal uniform for an event like this, but somehow the fatigues suited him—made him look more like Jack.

Her hands were shaking slightly as she set them on the podium, waiting for the professor and Jack to leave the stage. She tried to still her thoughts and let her professional face slide into place. She'd always been bothered with nerves. It was weird. Put her in a clinical situation—even an epidemic—and she could deal with the pandemonium of that no problem. Put her in a classroom setting, or even an interview setting, and her heart would race at a million miles an hour, making her thoughts incoherent and her words even worse. She'd had to work at this. She'd had to work hard.

She took a few deep and steadying breaths. Truth was, she could do this presentation in her sleep. She knew the information inside out. But could she present with the commitment and compassion that Jack just had? He was a hard act to follow.

A horrible queasiness came over her. That familiar feeling of not being good enough. The way she'd constantly tried to prove herself to her father by getting perfect grades, being the first in her class, qualifying for med school—all just to gain a second of his attention. Those memories ran deep—even though her father was gone. She hated feeling this way. And as she looked out over the sea of expectant faces, she felt her anger spike.

She looked up as Jack descended the stairs to her right. At the last possible second he turned his head, gave her a cheeky grin and winked at her. *Winked at her.*

A little spurt of adrenaline raced through her body. The cheek. Right now, she could cheerfully punch him. Anything for an outlet to the bubbling frustration she was feeling inside.

She lifted her head and looked out at the still-waiting audience. She could do this. She could. She could be good enough. She could deliver her presentation with the same passion and commitment as he had. She would deal with Jack Campbell later. She tilted her chin upward and plastered her most professional smile on her face. "Thank you so much for inviting me here today…"

So her name was Amber Berkeley. It suited her. A tiny bit quirky, with a hint of grace.

He'd had no idea she was a speaker at the conference. That was the thing about not sharing names and trying to be a little mysterious—it made you miss out on other things.

He'd left the stage and stood at the back of the auditorium listening to her. Her nerves were clearly evident. Her hands had been shaking and she'd been white as a ghost as she'd stepped up to the podium. Last night she'd been brimming with casual confidence. He'd liked that better.

But as he'd stood and watched, the woman he'd

met last night had slowly emerged. It was clear she knew and understood her subject matter. She spoke eloquently about meningitis and its spread, the way that the different viruses adapted and changed and the problems that could cause. He was impressed with the way she handled random questions that were thrown at her about the new emerging types of meningitis and the difficulties in diagnosing quickly enough for appropriate treatment.

He'd learned something new. And as she stepped down from the podium and walked back up the aisle toward him, he waited for her at the door, pushing it open as she approached.

The light in the foyer was bright compared to the auditorium. She stepped outside, blinked for a few seconds then unfastened her jacket and breathed a huge sigh of relief.

"You winked at me, you cheeky…" She left the last word missing.

"Did I?" He raised his eyebrows.

She shook her head and sagged against the wall for a second. "Thank goodness that's over."

He looked surprised. "You were good. What on earth were you worried about?"

She arched an eyebrow at him. "Who said I was worried?"

"Do your hands normally shake?"

Her tongue was stuck firmly inside her cheek. She waited a second before replying, then pulled her shoulders back and started to walk past him. "For that, you owe me breakfast. I couldn't eat anything earlier but right now I could probably eat the entire contents of the kitchen."

He held his arm out, gesturing toward the nearby hotel restaurant, trying not to fixate on the swing of her hips in that skirt. "Your wish is my command." Then he gave a little smile. "I seem to buy you a lot of food."

She tutted and shook her head as she walked past him, letting one of the waiters show them to a table looking out over the Pacific Ocean. The wind had whipped up outside, bringing the earlier dark clouds closer and making all the parasols on the beach shake.

Amber glanced outside. "What's that all about? I came here for sunshine and good weather."

Jack shrugged. "Almost looks like a day in Scotland instead of Hawaii. Must just be in for a bit of bad weather."

Amber sat down quickly as the waiter showed them to a table. She didn't hesitate to order. "Can I have coffee, please? Not just a cup—a whole pot. And some eggs, sunny-side up, and some rye toast, please."

Jack gave a nod and tried not to smile again. "I'll have what she's having—and some orange juice, please." He waited until the waiter had left. "So, you didn't want to hear the next speaker?"

She laid her hand on her stomach. "Are you kidding? If I'd stayed in there I'm sure all five hundred delegates would have heard my stomach rumbling. I had to eat."

Her hair was tamer today, tied back in a slick ponytail instead of piled haphazardly on top of her head. The pink tips were just visible when she turned her head. The simple black suit and white shirt were elegant, but as they sat at the table, she pulled off her jacket and rolled up her shirtsleeves midway, revealing a host of gold bangles.

"You ducked out on me."

She looked up quickly. For the briefest of seconds she looked a bit startled, but he could almost see her natural demeanor settling back into place. "How do you know I ducked out? You were too busy snoring."

He shook his head. "I don't snore. You, however..."

"You never told me you were a doctor." The words were almost accusing.

"Neither did you."

For a second she didn't speak. It was almost like a Mexican standoff.

He could see her swallow, and then she gave him a haughty stare. "I don't mix with fellow doctors."

Jack leaned forward. "What does that mean?" He held out his hands. "And what do you call this?"

"This," she said firmly, "is breakfast. Breakfast is fine."

He kept his elbows on the table, wondering if he could lean even closer. "Oh, so I can buy you food. But you can't spend the night with me?" He wanted to laugh out loud. She sounded so uptight, and that seemed a total turnaround from the woman he'd met last night.

But now he was curious. "So, what exactly is wrong with doctors? After all, you're one."

She gave an exasperated sigh. "I know. It's just…" He could see her try to find the words. "It's just that I don't like to mix work with…" She winced.

"Pleasure?" He couldn't resist.

She closed her eyes for a second.

He sat back in his chair and folded his arms. "So, if I'd told you last night in the bar I was a doctor, you wouldn't have come back to my room with me?"

She bit her bottom lip. He could tell she knew she was about to be challenged.

"Well, yes."

He held open his arms. "It's a conference full of medical professionals. The hotel is full of them. Who did you think you might meet in the bar?"

She shrugged. "There's more than one conference on in this hotel. I thought you were maybe one of those—" she waggled her hand "—business, economic-type guys."

He let out a laugh. He couldn't help it. From the second he'd started studying medicine it had felt as if he practically had *doctor* stamped on his forehead. He put his hand on his chest. "Me?

You honestly thought I was some kind of accountant, computer, business-type geek?" He shook his head. "Oh, my army colleagues would just love that."

She looked distinctly uncomfortable and he tried to rein in his amusement.

"Why are you getting yourself so worked up? Nothing happened. You know it didn't." He gave her a kind of sideways glance. "Maybe… if things had been different and jet lag hadn't been involved then we could be having an entirely different conversation today."

He was probably pushing things. But it was true. There had been a spark between them last night. He wouldn't let her try and deny it.

Her face was pinched; there were faint wrinkles along her brow. He couldn't actually believe it. She really, really did have an issue with the fact he was a doctor.

He'd worked with colleagues in the past who didn't like to mix work with relationships. It wasn't so unheard of. Maybe if he'd adopted that rule he wouldn't have ended up losing someone. He wouldn't have felt the need to shut himself off entirely from the rest of the world.

But even as he had that thought he knew it was ridiculous. Relationship or not, they would still both have been posted to Afghanistan. He'd been tortured with what-ifs for a long time before he realized nothing would have changed.

He saw a glimmer of something in Amber's blue eyes. A spark at his words. Baiting her was easy.

She flung her paper napkin at him. "No way."

He raised his eyebrows. "Purely because I'm a doctor?"

She neglected to answer that part of the question and gave him a long stare. "Let's just say had you been some mysterious businessman…" She leaned back in her chair and crossed her long legs. "It's a bit insulting, really."

Was she changing tack? He mirrored her actions and leaned back in his chair. "What is?"

"A man inviting you back to his room, then promptly falling asleep and ignoring you."

He squirmed. When he'd woken up this morning he'd cringed. He remembered sitting up in the bed together to eat their second burger and fries. He also remembered watching some old movie with her and laughing along at the lines.

And he could just about remember a warm body wrapped around his in the middle of the night. He'd tried not to remember the fact it had felt good because that flooded him with things he didn't want to acknowledge.

He lifted his hands. "Guilty as charged. Sorry. It was the jet lag." He put his elbow on the table and leaned a little closer. "But now? Jet lag is gone. Let's start again."

Even though she'd just tried to joke with him, she still looked the tiniest bit uncomfortable. She obviously took her "no fraternization with other medics" rule seriously. He couldn't help but be curious.

He waved his hand. "Relax, Amber. This is just breakfast. Nothing more. Nothing less. What do you have against fellow doctors, anyway?"

She didn't meet his gaze; she just sucked in a breath as her fingers toyed with the cutlery on the table. "Let's just say I lived in an environment with an absentee medic who was obsessed with his work. As a child I had no choice. As an adult, it's not a situation I ever want to repeat."

He wanted to ask questions. He did. But somehow he got the impression it wasn't really the time. He was curious about this woman. And after two years, that was a first for him—one that he couldn't quite understand.

The waiter appeared with the coffee and filled up their cups. Jack decided to take things back to neutral territory. "You might have told me you were a speaker."

She raised her eyebrows. "You might have told me you were starting off the conference." She gave a thoughtful nod. "You were good. I was impressed." Her eyes ran up and down his uniform. "I can't believe I thought you were at the business conference. I should have guessed. Your suit didn't quite fit perfectly—and, let's face it, those guys probably spend on their suits what I would on a car. I should have guessed you were an army guy. I'm still surprised you didn't mention it."

"I'll try not to be insulted by the suit comment—because you're right. I much prefer to drive a reliable car than buy a fancy suit. If you want to split hairs, you didn't mention you worked for the Disease Prevention Agency. Aren't you guys supposed to walk about in giant space suits?" He grinned and nodded his head.

"Now I understand the comments at the bar about the peanuts."

She shuddered. "You have *no* idea what we've found on bar snacks."

He laughed as he kept shaking his head. "And I don't want you to tell me." This was better. This was more what he wanted. He could gradually see the tension around her neck and shoulders start to ease.

The waiter appeared with their eggs and toast, and Amber leaned over the plate and inhaled. "Oh, delicious. And just what I need."

She ate for a few minutes then looked back up at him. "Your wound dressing. It looks good. How on earth did you discover the science behind it?"

Jack was spreading butter on his toast. "There's been quite a bit of work on clot-forming dressings. My problem was they just didn't work quickly enough for the situations we were in. But—" he gave her a smile; she was watching him with those big blue eyes "—the Internet is a wonderful thing. I contacted a few people who'd led other studies and asked if we could try a combination. I knew the specifics of what

I really needed. I needed something so simple that it could be slapped on by anyone—and so quick acting it could stop bleeding within twenty seconds."

The glance she gave him was filled with admiration. "I heard people talking after you finished. They think you're sitting on a gold mine."

Jack shifted uncomfortably in his chair. "It's not about money," he said quickly.

Amber didn't even blink, just kept staring at him with that careful gaze. "I know. I got that."

He picked at his eggs with his fork. "I know that for a lot of people medicine is a business. Britain isn't like that. The army isn't like that. Our health care is free—always has been and hopefully always will be. I'm not sure I can exist in a climate where every dressing gets counted and every profit margin looked at."

She took a sip of her coffee. "You've already been approached, haven't you?"

He bit the inside of his cheek, unsure of how much to tell her. Jack liked being straightforward. And from what little he'd seen of Amber, she seemed to operate that way too. That thing on the stage had just been a wobble—he was sure.

"Right from the beginning we had a contract arranged and a product license developed. It was developed during army time, so they have a part ownership, as do the original creators of the components." He sighed. "I knew this could happen. As soon as I realized how good it was, I wanted to make sure that it wouldn't end up being all about the money. That's not why I did this—it's not why *we* did this. And I know it's good. I know it could save lives around the world, and that's what I want it to do."

She tipped her head to the side and studied him for a few seconds. "I like that." The color had finally returned to her cheeks and she seemed more relaxed.

He gave her a smile. "Your presentation was good too. I know the basics about meningitis but not the rest. I had no idea just how quickly the strains were mutating."

She pushed her plate away. "Thank you. The presentation was important. I'm the only person here from the DPA this time, and I wanted to be sure that I gave a good impression." Her fingers were still wrapped around her fork, which she was drumming lightly on the table. "Monitoring infectious diseases is all about good international working." She let out a little laugh. "Let's just say that some of our counterparts have been a bit reluctant to share information in the past. In a world of international travel it makes contact tracing interesting."

"Ouch." Jack wrinkled his brow. He couldn't imagine trying to contact trace across continents. It was bad enough on the few occasions he had to make an urgent call to a far-off relative, and that was with all the army resources at his disposal.

He topped up his coffee. "Want anything else to eat?"

She shook her head. "I think I'm done. Thank you for this."

She kept staring at him, with a hint of a smile around her lips. He waited a few seconds then couldn't help himself.

"What?"

This was odd. It was the most relaxed he'd been around a woman for a while.

But he liked this woman's sense of humor. He liked her sassiness. And he was curious about the hint of vulnerability he'd seen on the stage.

Not that it had stopped her—she'd gone on to deliver an impressive talk.

And he couldn't help but be curious about the No Doctor rule she'd obviously decided to follow.

There was a rumble outside and they both glanced out at the darkening and choppy ocean. "I thought Hawaii was supposed to be sunshine, sunshine and more sunshine." He frowned.

"Not forgetting the killer surf waves," she added as she kept her eyes on the ocean. "I think you were right. It looks like you brought Scotland's weather with you."

He shook his head. "Believe me, you wouldn't go into the sea in Scotland when it looks like that. Even on a roasting hot day, the sea still feels like ten below zero. On a day like today? You'd be a frozen fish finger."

She burst out laughing. "A what?"

He wrinkled his brow and drew a tiny rectangle on the table with his finger. "You know, cod or haddock, covered in bread crumbs. For kids. They're kind of rectangular."

"Oh…" She nodded. "You mean a fish stick."

The wrinkles grew even deeper. "A fish stick? What's a stick about it? It's a rectangle."

She folded her arms across her chest. "Well, what's a finger about it?"

He waved his hand in mock exasperation. "You Americans."

"You Scots," she countered just as quickly.

"Is this what we're going to do?" He couldn't help himself. He lowered his voice. The look she gave him through her thick lashes sent tingles across his skin.

"What do you mean?"

He gestured to the table. "Eat food and argue about words. We're starting to be a habit."

She glanced at her watch. "A habit? After less than twenty-four hours? Has to be a new world record."

He leaned his head on his hand. He really should go back in to the auditorium and listen to some of the other talks. He should be thinking about his career, and be circulating and making contacts the way he'd failed to last night. But somehow, like last night, the only contact he was interested in making was right in front of him.

Three days in Hawaii. That was how long he

planned to be here. He could easily lose himself in three days with a woman like Amber Berkeley. She was smart. She was fun. And he could sense the spark between them.

In a way he was glad nothing had happened last night. It meant their flirtation could happily continue and he could find out a little bit more about her. All within the confines of the conference. Whether they attended any more talks or not was entirely a different story.

As for her No Docs rule? Rules were made to be broken. And they didn't work together—never would. Maybe she could be persuaded to spend some more time together. His stomach gave the weirdest little lurch. He couldn't believe he'd actually just thought like that.

He'd imagined landing in Hawaii to scorching sun, colorful flowers and interesting birds and wildlife. That was the picture he'd always had in his head.

He'd lived so long in his own little bubble that finding someone to exchange anything other than clinical findings with was odd. But odd in a good way.

He looked her straight in the eye. "You've never just met someone and clicked?"

She blinked for a second as if she wasn't quite sure how to answer. "Is this a trick question?"

He shook his head. "What? No."

Then she tapped her fingers on the table slowly. "Okay, since you found out my name, did you look me up online?" She looked a little anxious.

He shook his head again. He was getting more confused by the second. "No. Why, should I?"

She hesitated for a few seconds then rolled her eyes and waved her hand. "There's no point hiding it. If you search up my name you'll find the whole news headlines. A very long time ago, when social media was a mere babe, and I was working as an intern, I met a fellow medic." She lifted her fingers. "And I clicked."

He folded his arms across his chest. "You clicked? Oh, no. You're not getting away with that. What happened to the No Doctors rule?"

She sighed. "Let's just say this was a huge contribution to the No Doctors rule."

"Tell me more."

She gave a slow rueful nod and held up her hands. He couldn't quite work out the expression on her face; it was a mixture of sad, exasperated and just…tired. "I was duped, I admit it. Or I was *charmed*."

"How charmed?" He was definitely curious. Amber didn't seem like the kind of girl to be either duped or charmed. Maybe there was a reason for the slightly brash exterior?

"Charmed enough to plan a wedding." She stopped for a second. "My father was a very accomplished surgeon, notorious for only picking the best of the best for his residents. He was also notoriously sexist. There were no women on his team. Charles used me, to get to him." The words were matter-of-fact, but the way that she said them wasn't.

"He did?" Jack couldn't help the wave of disgust that swept over him and the way his heart twisted a little for her. "So what happened?"

She shrugged. "I found out on the morning of the wedding via an overheard conversation in the local hairdresser that he'd been boasting about getting on my father's team, and worming his way in through me."

"I thought women were supposed to drink champagne on the morning of their wedding."

"Oh, I was drinking champagne as they pinned my hair up. I thought about it all the way home. I thought about it all the time I stepped into my dress and little things came into my head, like a giant jigsaw puzzle slotting into place. By the time I reached the church and saw him standing at the top of the aisle, the smug expression on his face told me everything I needed to know. I turned on my heels, picked up my dress and ran."

"You ran?" He couldn't actually believe it.

She gave a small nod. "Do an Internet search of Milwaukee Runaway Bride. That's me." A long slow breath hissed out from her lips. "Not really something I want to put on my résumé." Her eyes looked up and met his. She gave a half shrug. "I hate the thought of people reading that about me online. It's like a permanent stain on my character."

She put her hands up to her forehead as if it ached, closing her eyes for a second. It was obvious she found this hard.

But she was being honest. He appreciated that. What would he have thought if he'd read this online? Probably, that she was a bit of an idiot, or that she was an attention seeker. Hearing it in person from her was an entirely different experience. He could tell that the whole experience had changed her.

"Regrets?" The words were out before he really thought about them, but Amber quickly shook her head as she lifted it from her hands.

"No. My father never spoke to me again. Nor did Charles. But then again, Charles lost his job the next day."

"You never spoke to your father again?"

She shook her head again but didn't look sad. Her words were more assured. "No. I was the ultimate disappointment. But then again, no matter how well I did, I'd always known that."

He could almost see her physically bristle.

"What kind of surgeon was he?"

"Renal. Top of his game—until the day he died."

"He wasn't proud that his daughter was a doctor too?"

"Don't think he even noticed." Her answer was short and snappy. "Truth was, I wasn't a boy. By the time I realized how little respect my father had for me, and my mother, I was done with him anyhow. He died a few years later and it actually set my mother free."

Jack was a little surprised at her words but at least now he had half an understanding about her No Doctor rule. Of course, it didn't make sense. But in her head, it did.

Then she took a deep breath and shook her head. "Let's change the subject." It was clear there was a lot more to this, but he could tell that she'd shared enough, and he respected her for that.

Her blue eyes met his and she sat up a little straighter in her chair, tilting her head at him. It was like a shock wave. When the anger and resentment left her face, Amber Berkeley was stunning. "You said last night you should probably be schmoozing. You're almost not in the army now. What's your plans, soldier?"

He raised his eyebrows. "Why, are you offering me a job?"

She straightened her back and narrowed her gaze, imitating some kind of stern interviewer. "Well, let's see. I know your qualifications. I know you're from Scotland. I know you appear to be quite bright, and maybe even a little bit of a humanitarian." She put her elbows on the table and leaned toward him. "Think you could cut it at the DPA?"

He gave a lazy kind of smile. "Not if you call chips fries."

She sighed and waved her hand. "Oh, well, that's it. Interview fail. I'm sorry, Dr. Campbell—looks like you have to work on your interpersonal skills."

He nodded in agreement. In the corner of the room one of the conference staff had a phone in her hand and was talking quietly to one of the waiters and pointing toward their table. After a few seconds she approached. "Dr. Berkeley?"

Amber turned around in surprise. "Yes?"

"Would you mind taking a call from one of your colleagues from the DPA?"

Amber stared down at her bag for a few seconds, and then her face crumpled. "Darn it. I switched off my phone before I came down because I knew I'd be in the auditorium. I hope nothing is wrong."

She held out her hand for the phone. "This is Dr. Berkeley." He heard it instantly. The change in her tone, her professional persona slipping back into place. He wondered if he should move to let her take the call in privacy, but she didn't seem to mind the fact they were still sitting together.

"Hi, Warren. Yes. No. Really?"

He watched as he could see her concentrating. After a few seconds she fumbled around in her bag. Jack reached into his fatigues and pulled out his pocketbook and pen, pushing them across the table toward her. She nodded gratefully as she flicked open the book and started to scribble. "Yip, what's the name? Oh…how awful. Which strain? Yes. Do you have a contact at the local agency? At the admitting hospital? Okay. Can Drew give me a lab contact I can work with? I might have more experience at identifying the strain. Sure, no problem." She glanced outside at the darkening sky. "No." She gave a little smile, then met his gaze. "Things have been a little different than expected. Let me get on this." She clicked the phone and sighed as she set it down on the table.

"Something wrong?"

She nodded. "A new unidentified strain of meningitis. One affected teenager. A request for assistance has been made to the DPA and since I'm here…"

She let her voice tail off. Jack spoke carefully. "It's your specialty area—of course they should call you."

She nodded. "I know. I'm lucky it's meningitis. In the DPA you have to do a bit of everything. I've been in Africa looking at polio and sleeping sickness, Chicago, when we thought we might have a smallpox outbreak, and Washington and Texas for flu." She gave a resigned kind of smile. "We get all over." She stared over toward one of the windows. "Let's just hope it's only one case. I'm here by myself. If there's any more and it turns into an outbreak, contact tracing could be a nightmare."

It was all he needed to hear and he made his mind up instantly. Jack was never going to schmooze his way around this conference trying to find a suitable job. No matter how much his head told him he should, it just wasn't in him to do it. He couldn't do it. He was far more interested in finding out more about the woman sitting opposite him. It had been so long since he'd felt like this. She was sparking his interest in so many ways—so many ways that he hadn't acknowledged in such a long time. He stood up. "Okay, then, let's go."

Amber's eyes widened. "What?"

He shrugged. "No point in you going alone. And I guess you could always do with another pair of hands even though it's not my specialty. If it turns into more than one case, you'll need help. I can be that help. Why don't you change, I'll grab a few things from my room and I'll meet you back down here in ten minutes?"

Amber looked a bit lost for words. She waved her hand toward the doors to the foyer. "But don't you have to work the room, find a job?"

"I just flunked my last interview." He gave her a wink. "I've been told I need to work on my people skills. No time like the present to start."

She stood up and picked up her bag. "Are you sure about this?"

He gave the briefest of nods. "Let's face it. You're the most interesting person I've met here. Better stick around."

He could swear that was relief on her face. "Okay, then, Dr. Campbell. I'll meet you in ten."

* * *

She'd never changed so quickly—just kicked off her heels and let her expensive suit crumple across a chair. She pulled on a pair of stretchy dark trousers, a short-sleeved shirt and a pair of flats. Because her wardrobe was mainly formal clothes for the conference—none of which she wanted to wear to the local hospital—she grabbed her least formal jacket, a khaki military-style one. She shook her head as she pulled it on. At this rate, she and Jack would look like a matching pair.

She dumped her purse and stuffed her wallet, phone and notebook into a small backpack. She'd learned over the years to travel lightly.

She still couldn't believe he'd volunteered to come with her but she was secretly pleased. It didn't matter that she was confident in her practice. It didn't matter that she'd handled contact tracing for meningitis on numerous occasions. This was the first time she'd actually represented the DPA on her own. And it made her a tiny bit nervous. But from what little she knew of Jack Campbell, she hoped he would have her back.

He was already waiting as she walked back out to the main foyer. It was busier than she'd expected. Filled with anxious faces. Jack was standing among some other people.

"What's happening?" she asked.

"Look at that rain."

"What did they say about a weather warning?"

"I've never seen black clouds like that before. What happened to the sun?"

Jack was still wearing his fatigues; for the second time she tried not to notice how well they suited him. He smiled as he noticed her similar garb. "Are we ready to get started? I think we should move. Something seems to be happening."

She nodded. "We need to go to the Hawaii Outbreak Center and Lahuna State Hospital."

They walked across the foyer and out to the hotel main entrance. Both of the suited doormen were standing inside. They looked at her in surprise. "What's your destination?"

Almost immediately the sharp wind whipped her ponytail around her face and she had to brace her feet to the ground. She glanced around as her jacket and shirt buffeted against her. Rain thudded all around her, bouncing off the ground. The streets were almost empty and she could feel the stinging sand on her cheeks picked up from the beach across the road. All of the straw beach umbrellas had tipped over and were rolling precariously around. No one seemed keen on rescuing them.

Hawaii had never looked like this in any of the photographs she'd seen.

The doorman looked down at the deserted street. When she'd arrived the day before it had been packed with cars and taxis.

He gave a wave. "Come back inside and I'll call for a car. It may take a while. We've just had a six-hour emergency hurricane warning. The hotel is just about to make an announcement. All residents are going to be asked to stay inside. Could your journey wait? It's unlikely flights will be taking off anytime soon."

"What?"

"What?"

Jack's voice echoed her own. A wave of panic came over her. Did this mean she couldn't get to her patient?

She shook her head. The doorman was obviously assuming the only place people would try to get to right now was the airport. "I'm a doctor. I have to go to the Hawaii Outbreak Center then Lahuna State Hospital. I have to consult on a meningitis case."

The doorman gave her a solemn nod and didn't try to put her off any further. "Give me five minutes. I can get my brother-in-law to pick you up." He drew in a deep breath as he picked up a phone at his desk and dialed the number. "You might have to be prepared to lock down wherever you reach. Once we're on hurricane alert everyone is instructed to stay safe."

Jack stepped forward. "I knew that the weather was looking bad, but when did they issue the hurricane warning?"

"Just in the last ten minutes. It seems to have picked up force somewhere in the mid Pacific. Apparently the hurricane has taken an unexpected sharp turn. We usually have more time to prepare. All hotels have been contacted and the news stations are broadcasting instructions."

"Is it normal to be so late letting people know?"

The doorman shook his head. "We usually have between thirty-six hours and twenty-four hours to prepare. We have statewide plans for hurricanes, but the truth is, Hawaii has only been affected by four hurricanes in the last sixty years. Tropical storms? Oh, they're much more common."

Jack met her worried gaze. She'd been in crisis situations before, but usually for some kind of an infectious disease—not for a natural disaster. It was almost as if he could sense her fleeting second of panic. He put his hand at the back of her waist and nodded toward the doorman. "Thank you so much for doing this. We're only going out because we have to and we'll be happy to lock down wherever appropriate."

Ten minutes later a taxicab appeared. They watched as a few large gusts buffeted it from side to side on the road. The doorman handed them a card with numbers. "We'll be keeping an inventory of guests in the hotel as we do the lockdown. I've noted where you're going and here's some contact numbers if you need them. Good luck."

They climbed quickly into the back of the cab and Amber leaned forward to give the driver instructions. The roof of the hotel pickup point rattled above them. The driver listened to her then rapidly shook his head, gesturing toward the empty streets. "No. Pick one or the other. Which is the most important? We don't have enough time to take you to both."

Amber blew out a breath and turned to face Jack. "If the phones are still functioning I could call the Outbreak Center. It's more important to be where the patient and lab are, particularly if I want to try and identify the strain."

She didn't mind batting off him. It was always useful to throw ideas back and forward with another doctor and he had a completely different kind of experience from her—one that was more likely to be suited to this.

He nodded seriously as his eyes took in the weather around him. "Sounds like a plan."

She leaned forward to the driver. "Can you get us to Lahuna State Hospital?"

The driver nodded. "It's near the city center. We should get there soon."

The cab wove through the streets and high-rise buildings. There were a few people practically being carried along by the wind as they rushed to get places. Some stores were already closed, shutters down and all street wares brought back inside.

A large white building with dark windows emerged through the rain. The main doors and ambulance bay had their doors closed, with security staff visible through the glass. They unlocked the door as Jack and Amber jumped from the cab.

"We've had to close the automatic doors," one told her. "The wind is just too strong and a member of the public has already been injured."

Amber gave him a grateful smile as he locked the door behind them. "Can you direct me to Infectious Diseases? I've been called about a patient."

"Third floor. Elevators at the end of the corridor. Take a right when you get out."

The hospital was eerily quiet, the main foyer deserted as they made their way through. But as they reached the corridor in the heart of the hospital they could see uniformed staff swiftly moving patients and talking in hushed, urgent voices. "I wonder if the windows will be okay?" said Jack thoughtfully as they reached the elevators.

"What?" She pressed the button to call the elevator.

"The windows." Jack looked around him even though there were no windows nearby. "A place like this? It must have around, what—three hundred windows? How on earth do you police that in the middle of a hurricane?"

Amber blinked. She hadn't even thought about anything like that at all. "The hotel too. Do you think they'll tell people to leave their rooms?"

The doors slid open. "They must all have disaster plans. Won't they just take everyone to a central point in a building, somewhere they can hunker down?"

He could almost read her mind. Both of them had rooms at the hotel that they'd literally just abandoned with no thought to the impending hurricane. If they'd had a bit more warning she might have closed her curtains and stashed her computer and valuables somewhere safer. Who knew what they would return to later?

They stepped inside and she pressed the button for the third floor. It only took a few moments to reach there and the doors to the infectious disease unit. Amber reached for the scrub on the wall outside before she entered, rubbing it over her hands.

She could already see through the glass that the unit looked in chaos.

She turned to face Jack before she pressed the entrance buzzer. "Ready?"

She felt a tiny glimmer of trepidation. She was it. She was the sole representative for the DPA. Was she asking him, or herself?

But Jack didn't hesitate for a second. "Absolutely. Lead the way."

CHAPTER THREE

FROM THE SECOND she walked into the unit she was in complete control. He couldn't help but be completely impressed. Whatever the little waver was he'd glimpsed outside, it seemed to have disappeared. There were actually two infected patients. It seemed that they'd been brought in only a few hours apart. Was that the start of an epidemic?

Amber took it in her stride and reviewed them—Zane and Aaron, both eighteen, who were clearly very sick. Then she phoned the Hawaii Outbreak Center and liaised with their staff, and then asked for some instructions to find the lab.

Her face was a little paler as they headed to the stairs. "I need to find out what strain of meningitis this is. These kids have got sick really quickly."

The lab was down in the bowels of the hospital and they had to change into white lab coats and disposable gloves before entering. It was a modern lab, with traditionally white walls, an array of machinery and computers and wide work benches. But somehow it wasn't quite as busy as he might have expected.

"Where is everyone?" he murmured.

Amber shook her head as they walked through. "Maybe they've sent some staff home because of the hurricane warning."

The head of the lab was an older man, tall but thick and heavyset; he already knew they were on their way and walked over with his hand outstretched. "Mamo Akano. I take it you're my meningitis doctor?"

Amber nodded her head. "Amber Berkeley from the Disease Prevention Agency. Any further forward in identifying the strain?"

Mamo had deep furrows in his brow. "Maybe. The DPA just sent me some files over for you to consider. Come over here. I've opened them on the computer next to the microscope."

Amber hurried over and pulled up a stool next to the microscope. She glanced over her shoulder toward Jack. "Ready for this?"

It was the first time since he'd got here that Jack had felt out of his depth. This wasn't his forte. But he was always willing to learn. He gave a nod and pulled up a stool. "Tell me what you need me to do."

Three hours later her neck ached and her brain was fried. She'd spoken to her contacts at the Hawaii Outbreak Center, and her colleagues in Chicago. Their strain of meningitis seemed to be unique. It was definitely bacterial meningitis. The cerebral spinal fluid collected from both boys had been cloudy. But the gram stains hadn't given them the information that they needed. There was nothing like it on file—which was not entirely unusual, but just made things more difficult. It was closest to a previously identified strain of meningitis W135, but seemed to have mutated slightly. "What do we do now?" asked Jack.

Mamo sighed. He'd been by their side the whole time. "In theory, now we wait. But we can't really do that."

Jack frowned. "What do you mean?"

Amber gave a slow nod. "Mamo will need to

see what the most effective antibiotic for treating this strain is. But sometimes we don't know that for up to forty-eight hours—even seventy-two hours. We can't wait that long. Both of these patients are too sick. I need to try and treat them now."

Pieces clicked into place in Jack's brain. "So, you guess?"

"Yip," said Mamo, "Amber has to guess." His voice didn't sound happy.

Amber straightened up. Her voice was confident and her manner methodical. "Zane was already started on a broad-spectrum antibiotic—Penicillin G—when he was admitted. But it already looks like it hasn't started working. Neither of these boys was immunized. So, we immunize against Men W, and we treat them with something more specific—more than likely chloramphenicol—and hope the strain's not mutated too much." She pointed to the phone. "Let me make one more phone call. Then I'll go back up to Infectious Diseases to speak to the consultant. Then..." She turned to face Jack. "Then we're on a race against time. We need to contact trace. If there are children involved they may already have been immunized against meningitis W. But because this strain is slightly mutated, I still want to give them antibiotics. I can't take any chances with this."

"Meningitis W is one of the most dangerous strains, isn't it?"

She nodded. "That's why it was included in the immunization schedule in lots of countries only a few years ago. These kids really should have had this vaccine. But not everyone agrees with vaccination. Not everyone takes their kids for them, even though they can get them for free." She shook her head and turned to Mamo. "I need supplies. Where can I get oral supplies of antibiotics?"

Jack couldn't help but be impressed. She was on fire. This was her specialty and it was clear she knew the subject matter well.

Mamo walked over to another phone. "I'll talk to the hospital pharmacy. It's emergency circumstances—in more ways than one. Being part of the DPA will give you visiting physician credentials. You'll be able to get what you need."

She nodded again in grateful thanks. Jack got that. He was a medic too and part of the army.

And, although he was confident in his abilities and credentials, it didn't matter where you were in the world—most countries had their own conditions and registrations for being a doctor. The US had different regulations for each state, so sometimes it made things difficult.

She nodded and laid her hand on Mamo's arm as he waited for someone to answer the phone. "Thank you," she acknowledged. He nodded as they made their way back out of the lab and to the elevators.

She leaned against the wall as the elevator ascended. A few strands of her dark pink-tipped hair had fallen around her face and shoulders, and he could practically see the tension across her shoulders and neck.

He leaned forward and touched the end of one of her strands of hair. "I never asked last night. Why pink?"

She blinked for a second as if her mind was racing with a million different thoughts, then glanced sideways as she realized he was touching her hair. "Why not?" she replied simply.

There was something about the expression on her face that made him suck in his breath. She appeared calm and methodical. He was seeing Amber Berkeley at her best.

He was so used to being in charge. But here? Here, he was just Jack Campbell. This wasn't a trauma situation. Here, he had to let the person with the most experience lead the case. And that was hard for him. "What can I do?"

He had to ask. He wanted to help. He'd help any colleague who needed it—whether it was his specialty area or not. The army had made him adaptable in more ways than one.

She fixed him with her steady blue eyes and gave him clear instructions. "I need to get histories. I need to find out where these boys have been in the last few days in detail. I need to know every contact. I need names, addresses, dates of birth—contact details if they have them."

Jack licked his lips and asked the first question that had danced into his brain. "And if they are too sick to tell us?"

She grimaced. "Then we ask their family. Their friends. Whoever admitted them. This is a potentially deadly strain. We can't wait. There isn't time." She shook her head. "I don't even want to think about what doing this in the middle of a hurricane means."

He gave a swift nod and reached over to give her arm a squeeze. "I can do detailed histories. I haven't done any for a while, but I still remember how. Let's split it. You take one, I'll take the other and then we can check if there's any crossover."

She looked down at his hand on her arm and gave a weary kind of smile. "Thank you for this, Jack. You didn't have to offer, but I'm glad you did. Usually I'm part of a team. So outside help is appreciated."

"You okay?"

She nodded. "The meningitis stuff? I can do it in my sleep. The hurricane stuff?" She shook her head. "I don't have a single clue. I feel completely thrown in at the deep end."

She gave a smile as the elevator doors slid open again. "Remember your first shift as a resident when it seemed like everyone on the ward was going to die simultaneously?"

He let out a wry laugh. Everyone felt like that their first day on the ward. "Oh, yeah."

"It feels a bit like that all over again."

He gave her a smile. "Well, think of me as your

backup plan. You lead, I follow. Brief me. What do I need to know?"

She glanced over the notes she had. "Okay, these two kids were both part of a surf club. Zane became sick first, exhibiting some of the normal meningitis signs—high temperature, fever, signs of an early chest infection and, a few hours later, some confusion."

"So, there are at least a few hours between the disease progression in these kids?"

She gave a slow nod. "They were worried they might have to sedate Zane, but the lumbar-puncture procedure went smoothly and they started him on IV antibiotics straightaway."

"And the second kid?"

"Aaron came in a few hours after Zane with symptoms of shock. One of the other young guys had gone to see why he hadn't joined them and called 911 when he found him still in bed. The ER physician connected the cases pretty quickly. Neither of them had been vaccinated against Men W, and both had been bunking down at one of the local student residences."

Jack let out a slow breath. "Darn it. Close contacts?"

She nodded. "Close contacts. We need names and to find the rest of the kids who were in that residence."

"What else should I be looking for with close contacts?" He realized he was firing questions at her but he couldn't help it. He wanted to make sure he covered everything.

"The rules are generally people who've slept under the same roof, nursery or childcare contacts, and anyone they've shared saliva or food with. Dependent on age, they all need a two-day course of rifampicin."

Jack pulled a face. "Shared saliva with? You mean anyone they've kissed? For two teenage boys at a surf school we might have our work cut out. How far back do we need to go?"

"Seven days from first symptoms."

"Let's hope the surf school kept good records, then, and let's hope the boys know who they kissed."

The lights around them flickered and they both froze. "Please don't let us lose power," said Amber quietly. "This could be a disaster."

Jack sucked in a breath. He could tell the thought of the hurricane was making her nervous. Truth was, it made him slightly nervous too. But he had to believe that the authorities would have plans in place to take care of things. They couldn't control the weather. They also couldn't control time, and it was rapidly slipping away from them. "We have two cases. We can contact trace for these two cases and try and get antibiotics to anyone we think could be affected. Hopefully any younger kids will already be immunized."

Amber pulled a face. "Usually we would spend a few hours discussing this with the local outbreak center and the DPA. The impending hurricane doesn't help. What if we can't get to the people that need antibiotics? We can't ask people to leave their homes as a hurricane is about to hit. And who knows how long it will last?" She shook her head.

"It's a disaster," he said simply.

"Just pray it isn't an epidemic," she said swiftly. "Then it really would be a disaster."

By the time they reached the infectious disease unit again it was in chaos. Bed mattresses had been piled against the windows. The curtains around the beds had been taken down and also stretched across the windows with large Xs taped on the glass. A few of the patients who'd been there earlier had been moved out, but Zane and Aaron were still attached to all their monitors.

There was only one adult walking between both beds. Amber and Jack walked over to meet him. "I'm Amber Berkeley with the Disease Prevention Agency. Are you Zane or Aaron's parent?"

He shook his head. "Ty Manners from the surf school. They've both been with me for the last ten days. I can't believe they're both sick."

He glanced toward the covered windows and put his hands on his hips. It was clear he was stressed. "Everything has just happened at once. I should be down at the surf school making it ready—and sorting out the other kids."

Jack saw Amber word her question carefully. "Ty, I'm sure you're worried about all the kids in your care, and the surf school. Do you have any records? Do all the kids that go to the surf school stay in the same place? We really need to trace all the contacts that Zane and Aaron have had for the last seven days. It's really important we find out if other people have been immunized, and that we get some antibiotics to them if appropriate."

"It's definitely meningitis?"

Amber nodded. "It is. Both of their lumbar punctures were positive. And it's important that we treat things as quickly as possible. We don't want anyone else to get sick."

One of the nurses came and stood at Amber's shoulder with a clipboard in hand. "I've contacted both sets of parents. Zane's mother stays on Oahu. There's no way she can get here with the imminent hurricane weather but we're keeping her as up to date as we can. Aaron's mother and father live just outside Hilo. That's a two-hour drive to Kailua Kona. State police have told them not to leave their home but I have a horrible feeling they won't listen."

Amber walked over to the window and peeled back a tiny corner of the curtain. "Oh, my," she breathed as she looked outside.

The wind had picked up even more. Enormously tall palm trees were bending in the wind like drinking straws. Public trash cans were rolling down the street like empty soda cans. She watched as an awning at the café opposite was torn away before her eyes by the force of the wind and the red and white material disappeared like a kite being ripped from its string.

It made her heart beat a little faster. She turned to face the nurse. "How soon is the hurricane due to hit?"

The nurse glanced at her watch, then over to a TV screen they had in the corner of the unit. "In about an hour or two. It won't just be the winds. It will be the rain too. It's already started but this is nothing. Once it really hits we usually have floods. No one should be out there."

This was nothing? The rain she'd witnessed as they'd left the hotel had been bad enough. Even with the wipers at maximum their driver had barely been able to see out of the windscreen.

Amber spoke slowly. "But tell that to a parent that thinks their child is at risk." She closed her eyes for a second. "I wish I'd got a chance to speak to them. Maybe I could have played things down. Given them enough reassurance to wait."

Jack's voice was low. "But is that actually true? You suspect that this is an unknown strain of meningitis. The first antibiotics tried don't seem to hit the mark. Now it's up to the second. Are these boys really safe?"

Amber blinked back the tears threatening to appear in her eyes. "No," she said quietly. "Particularly when we don't know if our treatment is the right one. There's still a chance they could die—or have lifelong aftereffects."

She could see Jack's brain was trying to make sense of this all. His natural instinct as an army doc would be to prioritize. For a second there was a flash of something in his face. Something that made her step back. He looked as if he was trying to suppress his urge to take over. It was only the briefest of glances. But it brought back a surge of old emotions that she constantly felt around her father—as if she wasn't good enough for this. As if she couldn't possibly be good enough and someone like Jack, or her father, would have to step in and take over.

Her skin prickled. She hated that. Hated associating someone she'd just met with her father.

It wouldn't be the first time. She'd often met other doctors—particularly surgeons—who had the same old-fashioned attitudes and opinions. People who wanted to be in charge of everything—including her. These were the people she avoided wherever possible. Was Jack one of them?

Even that tiny flash of recognition in her brain would usually be enough to make her turn in the other direction. But in the circumstances, that was hardly possible.

The nurse interrupted her thoughts. "We're actually going to try and move these guys. They've done that in some of the other wards. Most of the corridors and central areas are full—and we have a lot of equipment we need to take. Someone is preparing a space for us down in the basement."

Jack's frown deepened. "Okay. We could help here. We should prioritize. Should we really be taking patient histories for close contacts right now when we might have no hope of reaching any of these people in the next few hours?"

Anger flared in her and Amber swallowed. She knew he was right. But she also knew how sick people could become with meningitis. She spoke in a low voice. "Jack, you offered to help. Not to take over. This is my specialty area, not yours. Of course I know this might be futile. But up until a few hours ago the hurricane wasn't heading in this direction. It might still turn. The prediction could be wrong."

Jack held his hands out. "Does it feel wrong to you right now?"

She held her nerve. She wouldn't let him tell her how to do her job. "Maybe not. But what if something happens to one of these guys? This might not be an epidemic yet—but it could be. It has the potential. And we have two young guys who've become really sick in only a few hours. What if something happens to one, or both, of them, and we've lost the opportunity to find their close contacts? What if we leave those people at risk? We also know this strain is slightly different. This could be the start of something." She pressed her hand on her heart. "I can't let the threat of a hurricane stop me from doing my job to the best of my ability. I have to take the histories. I have to collect the antibiotics and I have to try and talk to as many people as I can." She took a deep breath and her voice gave a little shake. "If the phone lines go down after this we could be in trouble. People might live near to medical centers. We can adapt. We could arrange for them to collect what they need from there."

His hands were on his hips. For a second she wondered if he was going to argue with her. Maybe bringing him here hadn't been a good idea after all. What did she really know about Jack Campbell? The army were used to being in the thick of things; maybe he was struggling with a back-seat role?

"I don't have time to fight with you about this, Jack. What are you going to be, a hindrance or a help?"

She could tell he was annoyed but she didn't have time to care. He had to do it her way, or no way.

There was a pause, and then he let out a sigh and gave the briefest shake of his head. "Let's be quick."

He grabbed a pile of paperwork and walked over to Aaron's bed. There was no chance of Aaron talking. He was ventilated with the brief-est hint of a purpuric rash on his tanned skin. The new antibiotics were feeding into an IV line. If they were going to make a difference they would have to start working quickly.

Jack looked up at Ty. "We're going to have to ask you questions because you've spent the last few days with these guys."

Ty gave a nervous nod. "Can't go anywhere anyhow. What do you need to know?"

Amber started firing questions at him. "Where did they sleep? How many other people are there? Do you have names, ages and contact details? Have any left in the last few days? How many are still there? How many people work at the hostel and at the surf school? What have they been doing at nights?"

Once she started she didn't stop. Every now and then Jack quickly interrupted with the words "And what about Aaron?" ensuring that Ty was answering for both teenagers.

It seemed that there were around twenty people at the surf school. Things were pretty informal. Most had traveled to get there—some from the other Hawaiian islands. The people who worked there were all local. Timescales were important. Two teenagers had traveled back to other states in the USA yesterday, and a third had left for New Zealand in the early hours of this morning.

While all this was going on, hospital staff

worked around them, attaching the two boys to portable ventilators that could be pushed out into the corridor with them; oxygen cylinders were attached to the sides of the bed and a portable emergency trolley was positioned near to the door.

One of the hospital administrators appeared and spoke in a low voice. "The patients in Surgical have been moved. The hospital front entrance has been completely cleared." Of course, it was covered in glass. "Medical CCU is the safest. It's right in the middle of the building with no windows, but we've already moved the sickest of our elderly patients in there. Pediatrics have been moved down to the theaters."

"Is the basement ready? Do you have the equipment that will be needed?" asked Jack. Transporting these patients would take more than the few nurses that were left in the department.

The administrator looked a little worried. "The staff room down at the laboratory has been cleared in the basement. The corridor down there is one of the most shielded in the building." The lights flickered around them again.

"As long as we don't have a power cut," said Jack warily.

"Let's go," said the head nurse smartly as the windows started to rattle around them. "I don't think it's safe to wait. We've packed up the equipment that we need."

She gestured to the nurses who were left. "You two with Zane." She looked at Amber. "You go with him too."

"Myself, Ty and Dr. Campbell will take Aaron down in the other elevator."

There was only one hospital orderly to assist— the rest obviously deployed to other parts of the building. How on earth did you lock down a hospital and keep all patients safe from a hurricane outside? She didn't even want to think about it.

They wheeled the bed out to the elevator, along with the portable ventilator, tanks and emergency trolley. The progress was slow; it was almost like a juggling act getting all the equipment they needed inside the elevator.

A few minutes later they arrived in the basement. This time she was familiar with the surroundings and backed out of the elevator first, pulling the bed with her. The lab staff must have been warned because a room to the right had been cleared. It looked as if it had been the large staff room, as a pile of chairs and large table were at the bottom of the corridor. The nurse guided the bed into the space and they quickly connected monitors to plug points and checked the ventilator was working properly.

It was weird. Amber actually liked being back in a hospital environment—even though this was a makeshift one. It always reminded her of why she did this job. Sometimes being stuck in an office at the DPA was tough. Only communicating with patients and fellow doctors by phone and email wasn't really how she preferred to work. She liked this. She liked being in the thick of things. She liked to see the patients, talk to them, be on hand when treatments were being tried and tested. A bit more like the role Jack had just done…

There was a weird sound from the corridor. The nurse looked up and frowned as she fiddled with some cables. "Go and check that, will you?"

The lights flickered again as Amber walked swiftly down the corridor. She automatically looked over her shoulder. It was like being in an old-style horror movie—never her favorite kind of entertainment.

The metal doors of both elevators were still closed. Shouldn't Jack be here by now with Aaron?

The lights flickered once more then went out completely.

Black. Everywhere.

She automatically sucked in a breath and held it.

"Darn it," came the shout from further down the corridor, followed by the flickering of some kind of light. Must be from a phone.

"You okay, Amber?" shouted the nurse. "We have a backup generator. It should kick in any second."

Something flooded into her brain. Keeping her hand on the wall, she walked quickly back to the room she'd just come from. The nurse had her phone in her hand and was using the light from it.

"Are the ventilators still working? Do we need to bag him?"

Even though it was dark, Amber moved to the bed, watching for the rise and fall of Zane's chest. The nurse was at the other side. She shook her head. "We should have three hours' worth of battery power. Honestly, the backup generator should kick in. Give it a few minutes."

There was a large thump from the corridor and some muffled voices shouting.

"Oh, no," said the nurse.

"What?" asked Amber.

"The elevator. I think your colleague's stuck in the elevator with Aaron."

Amber's heart started to thud in her chest. She lifted her hands from the bed. "Okay, you're okay here? I can go?"

The nurse nodded. Amber pulled her own mobile from her pocket and flicked the switch on as she walked back down the corridor.

The shouts were getting louder. "Jack? Are you okay?"

"Amber? Is that you? The elevator's jammed and the emergency phone isn't working!"

Amber ran over to the doors. It was ridiculous. She tried to pull them apart with her hands but it was obviously no use.

Mamo appeared from the lab. "Problems?" He

shook his head. "Can't do much without power down here."

She pointed to the doors. "We've got one of the kids with meningitis attached to a portable ventilator in there."

Jack shouted from inside. "Is there anything outside you could use to try and pry the doors apart? I can try from in here, but I think I need you helping on the outside."

There was a strange sound from inside. Almost a whimpering. Oh, no. The nurse inside must be freaking out. Being trapped inside a black box wouldn't be most people's idea of a normal working day.

"Hold on." Amber held her phone up and tried to scan the corridor around them.

Something seemed to flick in Mamo's head. "Over here. I think there's an emergency fire ax next to one of the exits. Maybe we could use that."

Sure enough, on one of the walls there was an ax mounted in a red box behind a breakable panel. Mamo pulled his lab coat over his fist and broke the glass, grabbing hold of the ax.

"Give us a minute, Jack," Amber shouted.

"Mamo is trying to pry the doors from this side." Something flashed through her brain. "Where's Ty?"

The reply was slightly muffled. "He stayed upstairs to make a few calls to the surf school. He wanted to check all the kids had been taken to an evacuation center."

Prying the doors apart was more difficult than it looked. Mamo put the edge of the ax into the gap at the doors and tried to turn it sideways to widen the gap. After a few minutes he turned to Amber. "You keep holding it," he said gruffly as he slid his hands and foot into the space that was only a few inches apart.

Amber kept trying to turn the head of the ax wider, while keeping it in the space. Her shoulder muscles ached. Her jaw was tight. From the other side she could see a flash of light. The nurse inside must be using her phone. White knuckles appeared on the inside of the door. She could hear the grunts and groans from Jack. "Grrr…"

After a couple of minutes the doors started to release a little further; both Mamo and Jack stuck their shoulders and body weight in the doors, using their feet to push the opposite door apart.

The elevator wasn't completely aligned with the floor—probably the reason they'd had so much difficulty prizing the doors apart.

The nurse looked numb. Amber ducked inside and grabbed the end of the bed. "You get the ventilator," she said to the nurse. "There will be a bit of a bump as we push out."

Mamo and Jack stayed at their doors, holding them back with their body weight as they guided the bed through between them. The nurse jerked as the bed thudded the few inches to the floor, then steered the portable ventilator alongside. The lights flickered in the corridor again.

"Got everything?" checked Mamo. Jack nodded as he pulled out the emergency trolley and let it roll across the floor. The two of them glanced at each other, then gave a nod and both jumped. The doors slid back into place swiftly just as the lights flickered back on in the basement.

"Thank goodness," breathed Amber.

Mamo gave a nod of acknowledgment as he glanced at Aaron in the bed. "Everyone okay?

I need to go back to the lab and check the machines."

Amber, Jack and the nurse pushed Aaron into the room in the basement. It only took ten minutes to make sure he was safely set up alongside Zane and that the power supply was working as it should be. The IV infusions with fluids and antibiotics stopped pinging, as did the cardiac monitor and ventilator.

"We're good." The nurse nodded. "I've phoned one of the ICU doctors and they're going to base themselves downstairs with us." She gave a rueful smile. "Don't worry. I've told them to take the stairs."

Amber walked back over to where she'd abandoned her paperwork. She had to get back on task. Time was ticking.

This was her responsibility and she was in charge. "Jack, how do you feel about making some calls? Let's do the international ones first. I can give you numbers for the public health agencies in the countries our patients are heading to. Following the patients up will be their responsibility."

Jack gave a nod. That tiny little feeling she'd

had that he might want to take over seemed to flutter away. "Yeah, I'm not sure how long our phone lines will work. Let's try and do these as quickly as possible. Then we could look at the people who've returned to any of the surrounding islands. See if we can get someone local to prescribe and supply the antibiotics."

She was pleased. He was methodical and logical. Definitely what she needed right now. It was odd to think that last night she'd fallen asleep next to a man she barely knew and now she was working with him in a virtual blackout.

One of the nurses gestured to them. "There's an office over there. Why don't you go and try the phones?" She pulled her watch from her pocket. "According to this, we have about ten minutes before the hurricane hits."

It was like a chill rushing over her body. Should she be scared? Should she actually be terrified? She'd faced plenty of disease disasters, but never a natural one like this. "What happens next? What happens to everyone out there?" she asked the nurse.

"They've moved most of the tourists from the beach-front hotels into emergency shelters. Hawaii has a hurricane preparedness guide. Unfortunately we've not had the warning time that would normally be in place. Things have changed quickly."

There was a tiny wave of panic. "Is there anything else I should know about a hurricane?" She hated the fact her voice sounded high-pitched.

"There's a standard set of instructions." One of the nurses pulled a leaflet from her bag.

Stay indoors away from windows, skylights and glass doors.
Secure and brace exterior doors. Store as much water as you can.
Close interior doors and take refuge in a small interior room, like a closet or hallway, on the lowest level of your home.

Jack pulled a face. "How do these apply to a hospital?"

The nurse gave a nod. "We've moved all the patients away from windows, mostly to the central corridors, and we've evacuated the top floor and ground floor. We're filling the baths and sinks with water to keep the toilets flushing, but the kitchen says it has ample supplies of drinking water." She closed her eyes for a second. "After that—we pray. This hospital has been standing for thirty years. We've had a few hurricanes in that time. We just hope that it will hold together again."

Amber gulped. "What about the staff? Do you all have to stay?"

She wasn't thinking about herself. She was thinking about all the local staff that might have families of their own close by to worry about. With the emergency warning coming so late, most of them might not have had time to make plans.

The nurse held out her hands. "We'll manage. The hospital has an emergency plan. Extra staff get called in as relief. They help transfer the patients and stock the ER. Some of the rest of the staff had to go home to sort out family issues. I came in early to let my friend go home to her disabled mother." She pointed at the nurse dealing with Aaron. "Nessa only started here a few weeks ago. Her family are on Oahu. She wouldn't have time to get there, so decided just to lock down here where she could be useful."

She gave an anxious glance between Amber

and Jack. "No matter what your experience, after the hurricane hits, we'll need doctors. Probably more than you know."

Jack gave the briefest of nods. His face was serious, but he didn't seem intimidated at all. "I'd rather be working than holed up in the hotel. Let us sort out what we can about these meningitis cases. After that, put me where you need me."

The nurse gave a nod. "I'll phone up to the ER and let them know we might have some additional help." Her eyebrows rose a little in question. "What will I tell them?"

His voice was firm. "Tell them I'm an army doc and can deal with whatever they need." His eyes met Amber. "Dr. Berkeley works for the DPA. She'll help out where she can."

"Great." The nurse picked up the phone and turned her back on them.

Amber gulped. For infectious diseases she was fine. But she wasn't quite as confident as Jack at being thrown in at the deep end. It wasn't that she didn't feel capable. She would always help out in an emergency. She wasn't sure how qualified or equipped she'd be to deal with things. She'd never really worked in an ER setting. She'd been part of team expeditions for the DPA. But she'd never been in charge. Never had the full responsibility herself. But those expeditions had been more coordinated. She'd always ended up working in pre-ready emergency clinics or vaccination hubs.

Her director had already mentioned he thought she was ready to try her hand as a team leader on a field mission to further her experience. But this was entirely different—totally out with her normal expertise. It was almost as if Jack sensed something from her. He leaned over and whispered in her ear. "Don't worry. I've got your back."

Then he did something completely unexpected. He turned her toward him and lowered his forehead onto hers. It was a gesture of security. Of solidarity. Of reassurance.

Warmth spread through her. She looked up and met his gaze. His dark brown eyes were fixed on hers. They were genuine and steady.

She pressed her lips together and took a deep breath, so many thoughts flooding into her mind. Her brain was such a mess. All she could concentrate on was the feel of his hands on the tops of her arms and the gentle way his forehead pressed against hers. His warm breath danced across her skin. Her gaze was naturally lowered and she could see the rise and fall of his chest.

He was a doctor. The type of guy she'd spent most of her life trying to avoid any romantic entanglements with. And this was crazy. She'd already seen a flash of something in him that reminded her of the focused way her father used to be.

So, if she already had alarm bells flashing in her head, why wasn't she running for the hills? She could pretend it was the hurricane. That the only reason she wasn't moving was because she was stuck here.

But that wasn't what was anchoring her feet firmly to the ground.

That wasn't what was letting the heat from the palms of his hands slowly permeate through her jacket and trickle its way through her body. Her last few boyfriends had been as far removed from medicine as possible—a landscape gardener, then a chef. But somehow she hadn't felt this. This connection.

And she couldn't understand it. She'd only met

Jack last night. And yes, they'd clicked. There was no doubt the man was attractive. There was no doubt her mind was imagining so many other places they could go.

But the timing wasn't right. It wasn't right at all. Her mother's face flashed into her head. The tired, weary look that had always been visible. The sadness when she'd glanced at a clock and realized Amber's father wouldn't be home that night. The endless amount of wasted dinners scraped into a trash can. The times when Amber had sat at the dinner table, desperate to tell her father about her day, and he could barely pay attention—talking over her as he launched into yet another story about work, or surgery, or research. Or when he left the table again as soon as the phone had begun to ring with another call from the hospital.

She'd spent her whole life feeling like an unimportant spare part. Constantly trying to earn the approval of a man who barely knew she existed. When Jack had spoken on the stage earlier on today, he'd had the same conviction, the same passion and dedication as her father.

She sucked in a breath as she realized the similarities between them both.

Having any kind of relationship with Jack Campbell was a complete nonstarter. She'd already lived part of her life being second best in someone's life. She was determined never to allow herself to be in that position again.

She wanted to step away. She should step away.

But for the briefest of seconds her eyes just fixated on the rise and fall of Jack Campbell's chest under his fatigues. She tried to focus. She had a purpose. She was a physician. She was here as the representative of her agency. She had a job to do. She could continue to monitor Zane and Aaron to try and keep them stable. To chart the progress of the infection and its reaction to treatments. Information like this was vital right now—nearly as vital as stopping the potential of any spread.

Aaron's parents might be on the road here and in the path of the hurricane. Her skin prickled. The logical part of her brain told her that these people were Hawaiians. They would know all the emergency plans for hurricanes. They would know how to keep safe. But would they follow their heads or their hearts?

Two years ago she'd had to make a heartbreaking call to another parent. She'd been called to an ER overwhelmed with flu patients. A small child had been admitted straight from school with a history of asthma, difficulty breathing and a high temperature. She'd called the parents and told them they should attend as quickly as possible. They never got there. In their sense of panic they'd been involved in a car accident and it had etched a permanent memory in Amber's brain and a scar in her heart. If she'd said something different, maybe if she hadn't let them know the urgency that she was feeling, they might have taken more care.

But the truth was, in the midst of a chaotic ER, she'd held that little girl's hand—angry that the parents hadn't got there in time—and tried to assist as they'd attempted to resuscitate her. They'd failed. And then she'd got the news about the parents.

No one had blamed her. No one had needed to. She'd blamed herself.

There were always going to be tough times

being a doctor. She knew that. She expected that. But this one had hit her harder than others.

And it had affected her more than she'd realized. Her confidence at work and around others was mainly just bravado. It also helped her erect a shield around herself.

Her heart wasn't safe. She didn't feel in a position to form relationships. Not while she felt like this. Not when she couldn't open herself up to others. It was safer to be single. Safer to surround herself with colleagues who didn't seem to recognize her detachment, but, instead, thought of it as self-assuredness and confidence.

She told them she didn't date colleagues and let them think that her life was full of a hundred other potential suitors at any time of the day.

She didn't tell them that she'd run out of series to watch on her paid Internet TV.

For the briefest of seconds earlier today she'd thought she'd recognized something on Jack's face.

That expression. That look. A flashback—a haunting. It was momentary. Only lasting a few seconds.

But it made her feel *something*. A connection.

And even though there was a hurricane outside, that scared her more than anything. So she turned on her heel and walked away.

CHAPTER FOUR

HE WASN'T ENTIRELY sure what was going on. Maybe he'd been too forward with the woman who'd shared his bed last night. He'd wanted to envelop Amber in a hug, but her demeanor had told him not to, and he'd ended up just pulling her toward him and gently touching heads.

He still couldn't work out what had possessed him. He hadn't held a woman that close in… how long?

Two years. Two long, hard years.

One minute she was there. Next minute she was gone.

Jill Foster had been a bright-eyed medic he'd met in Afghanistan. She was one of the best he'd worked with. As a teenager she wanted to be a doctor but couldn't afford to go to university, so she joined the army instead. Her skills and natural talent were picked up and she excelled in her role.

They worked side by side for six months. And as soon as he got home he missed her. By the time they redeployed again they were dating. Right up until the day he was felled by abdominal pain. The bothersome ache that had been distracting him had turned into an acute pain and he'd collapsed after finishing a long emergency surgery. Twelve hours later he'd woken up and life had changed.

Life had changed completely.

He'd had an appendectomy. It seemed that the army doc hadn't recognized his own appendicitis. But in that twelve hours there had been an emergency—a group of soldiers had been caught in some cross fire and had needed to be retrieved. He was usually part of the emergency call-out team. But, when he'd been under anesthetic, Jill had taken his place. And it had cost her her life. While going to pick up their injured comrades the vehicle had driven over an IED, the effect instant.

Gone. Just like that.

He'd never forget the face of the base commander who'd been there to tell him as soon as he came around from anesthetic. The guy looked ill, his face pale underneath his tanned skin. The other soldiers had been retrieved, but Jill and three other members of the team Jack normally worked with had been wiped out.

The numbness spread through his body immediately. He pushed up from the gurney, ignoring any wound pain, and staggered across the compound toward the mortuary. Two squaddies saw him and ran over to help, throwing their arms around his waist to keep him steady.

But no one would let him see Jill.

And he knew why. He did. Surgeons knew better than anyone what the effects of an IED could be.

So, he sat on the floor of the mortuary for the next six hours and vowed to make his time in Afghanistan meaningful.

Everything after that became about the wound dressing.

Wartimes were tough. Surgeons dealt with explosive injuries that no normal surgeon would ever see. And because of his postings he'd grown familiar with the faces around the camp. The cheeky squaddie in the armory. The quiet Yorkshire lad who liked to read books. The gung-ho female sergeant who could give any guy a run for his money. All of them had ended up on his table.

Not all of them had lived. But Jack had done his best. He agonized over any person that he lost. Replayed everything in his mind, wondering what he could have done differently—could have done better.

Once he was in the desert setting, work was everything. He became almost obsessed. The research too was entirely in his focus. He quickly realized how good their dressing worked and what the life-saving implications were. It was everything to him.

It gave him something to focus on. It allowed him to build a shell around himself and close out the rest of the world. He still went above and beyond for his colleagues—he always would. But he'd lost the connection, he'd lost the emotion and empathy that he'd always had within the job.

He'd lost a little part of his heart.

And now? He had no idea what he was doing—in more ways than one. He wasn't worried about helping after the hurricane. The infectious disease stuff was beyond his professional expertise. But if he had to hunt down people to deliver emergency antibiotics, he could live with that.

What he wasn't so sure about was the fact that the first woman he'd held in two years had just blanked him and walked away. Was his heart so numb that he couldn't pick up on female cues anymore?

Amber looked as if she was sucking in some deep breaths as she scrubbed her hands at one of the sinks. The noise seemed to echo around them in the basement. He couldn't stand it. Should he apologize for holding her?

He shook his head and stalked across the corridor to the other room. The IV antibiotics were feeding slowly through to both Zane and Aaron. Both of them were still sedated and ventilated. He glanced at the monitors and then at their charts. The nurse came over and stood with him at the end of Zane's bed. She gave her head a slight shake. "I still don't know if he's reacting to the medicines. He still seems so flat." She gestured toward the rise and fall of his chest.

Jack nodded. He understood what she meant. All of Zane's accessory muscles were working around his chest area. With ventilation and sedation he should be in a much more stable position. It was almost as if his body was fighting against everything.

Aaron seemed much more settled. His heart rate, temperature and blood pressure were good. It seemed that he was reacting better to the treatments and medications.

The lights flickered again and the television monitor in the room across the hall shorted out. The nurse's face paled. "This is it," she said warily. "The TV signal is gone. The hurricane is about to hit."

Amber appeared back in the doorway. She looked awful. "What do you do next?"

The nurse gave the briefest shake of her head. "Hunker down."

For the next four hours they held their breaths as they waited to see if they would come out the other side of the hurricane. It didn't matter they were in the basement with no windows or possibility of flying glass. At times the whole foundation of the building seemed to shudder and Jack wondered if the whole hospital could end up on top of them. Doors and windows throughout the hospital must have been affected as the doorway to the stairwell at the end of the corridor continued to rattle incessantly. It was impossible to stay still for four hours. They had patients to look after, and Jack couldn't help but worry about the patients above them and the people outside. They tiptoed around each other in a kind of unspoken frustration. The phone lines had died. Between them they'd managed to reach fourteen of the local people who had stayed overnight in the same accommodation as Zane and Aaron.

"I thought the eye of the hurricane was supposed to be silent. Quiet even," he said to one of the older nurses.

She shook her head. "Maybe in a movie. Or in a fairy tale. I've only seen two hurricanes. And there was no silence. Except when they were over. We're being hit by the fiercest part of the storm right now. Anything or anybody out there right now probably doesn't stand a chance. Anything not anchored or cemented to the ground will likely never be seen again. Or end up on one of the other islands." She sighed, and he realized she must be thinking about her family on Oahu. He put his hand on her arm.

"I'm sure they're safe. Just like we are."

She gave the briefest of nods and then marched over to the monitors and started pressing buttons again. Jack was exasperated. He needed to be doing something. Anything. But he'd done everything he could down here.

Ty had been started on the antibiotics too. And he, in turn, had been concerned about his employees with young families.

Amber took the time to explain how meningitis passed from person to person and how, at the moment, unless an employee showed signs themselves, their families weren't at risk.

She seemed to circumvent Jack wherever he went. And that was fine. If he'd overstepped he was glad of the message.

They monitored Zane carefully, watching his limbs closely for any visible signs of septicemia. Eventually, Jack finally made his way up the stairwell to see if he could be of assistance in any other part of the hospital. He'd only made it to the first floor before he could hear the rattle throughout the building. The door at the stairwell had been juddering loudly, obviously being buffeted by wind that had found a way inside the hospital.

Jack stuck his head through tentatively. No patients should be on the first floor or the top floor. Flash flooding and roof damage were two of the major probable issues. The evacuation plan dictated that most patients were moved to central areas on the second and third floors.

"Hello?" he shouted. He concentrated and listened hard. All he could hear was the wind whistling through the building and the sound of thudding rain.

He pulled his head back in and started up to the second floor. There definitely would be patients and staff up there. There was a crowd of people in green scrubs standing at the entrance to the stairwell on the second floor. A few glanced in his direction as he pushed through. He held out his hand to the nearest member of staff with a stethoscope around his neck. "Jack Campbell, Senior Medical Officer, British Army. Can I do anything?"

He could see a myriad people in the corridors with swabs held to arms and heads. The man gave a brief nod. "Oh, yeah, the army guy. I heard about you. I'm Ron Kekoe. Head of the ER. We've had to move upstairs in case of flash flooding." He glanced at his watch. "We're going to give it a few hours then move back down, and send out teams as required." He pointed toward a makeshift desk just along the corridor. "Phones are down but we've got radios to contact other emergency services and the evacuation shelters." His face was serious. "We've already had a few reports of winds up to one hundred and eighty miles an hour and roofs being torn off buildings. There will be casualties." He frowned for a second and Jack realized someone had appeared beside him.

Amber, breathing heavily. She must have run up the stairs after him. His first thought was for the teenagers. "Zane? Aaron?"

She shook her head. "No. They're just the same. But I realized I probably wasn't much use down there. One of the residents is staying with them. I thought I should probably come and help."

He could hear it. That little edge of nerves in her voice. It was clear, however, that Ron didn't hear it. He just gave a nod. "The infectious disease doctor?"

Amber didn't seem to mind the label and held out her hand. "Amber Berkeley, DPA."

Ron gave her a half-suspicious look. "Someone mentioned you wanted to take antibiotics out." He shook his head fiercely. "No way. Not anytime soon. First vehicles that go out will be heading up portable trauma bays. If it's near to where you need to be, you're welcome to tag along—provided you do some doctoring."

He didn't even wait for Amber's reply. Jack got that. Everything about this was familiar territory to him. This was all about triage, all about prioritizing. Ron gave them both a nod. "Can you deal with some minor injuries? There's nothing too threatening. Just flying glass and debris. A few staff were caught. If you could clean and stitch that would be great."

Amber gave a quick nod of her head and walked around Jack, heading toward the first person with a bloody wound pad pressed to their forearm.

He watched for a few seconds as he could see

her swallow nervously. This was different for her. And he got that.

He moved on over and started treating the next member of staff who had a cut on their forehead.

He was methodical. And he was quick. All the injuries were relatively minor.

But as he worked steadily he noticed the continued chaos around him. Although the external phone lines weren't working, the internal phones rang constantly. Staff seemed to be disorganized, and Ron, as Head of the ER, seemed out of his depth.

Jack couldn't help himself. He walked over. "How about you let me do some of this?"

Ron looked up from a prescription he was writing. Three other members of staff were waiting to talk to him and the radio was crackling constantly on the table.

"What can you do?"

Jack pointed to the desk. "I have experience of crisis triage. How about I field all the radio calls? I can take the details and liaise with the other agencies. We need to know what's needed and where. As soon as the winds die down we could have teams packed up and ready to go. What do you say?"

He was trying so hard not to overstep. He could see Ron was struggling with the volume. He might not know Jack, but surely he would let him help?

Ron only paused for a few seconds as the radio continued to crackle.

"Perfect. Let me know if there's anything major."

"You got it." Jack settled at the desk and picked up the radio. There were a few notes already about building damage—but no reports about casualties. There was a footnote querying whether a home with disabled residents had been evacuated, with a note to check with the nearest evacuation center. There were a few other notes from a care agency who had several housebound residents that they hadn't been able to get to. Chances were they were safe. Most Hawaiians knew about the potential threats and what to do. But the infirm or frail would probably not have been able to put all preparations in place without assistance.

There seemed to be no standard way of keeping track of all the information, so Jack added all the names and addresses to a list for checks and pulled out a citywide map to start charting where everyone was.

Some staff were reporting that the sky was almost black now. No one with any thought to safety could possibly go outside.

The chatter on the radios was constant, along with the background noise of the hammering winds. Even though they'd been told not to, some of the staff squinted past mattresses at the windows and let out squeals and gasps. "Did you see that?"

"That car just flipped!"

"Oh, my, look over there. The roof's coming off that building like a tin can!"

"Those trees are bending like drinking straws."

"That one's going to snap for sure!"

The rain thudded off the windows, battering down in among the wind's fury. Debris flew through the air, randomly hitting windows and shattering glass.

Jack tried to tune it all out, focusing on the task he'd been given and trying to keep a clear head. But even though he tried, his eyes were distracted by the woman who'd pulled her hair back into a ponytail and seemed to be cleaning and stitching wounds precisely. She had a quieter nature when working with staff who were patients, and, even though he'd seen a smattering of nerves earlier today, he would never question her clinical skills.

Reports continued to come in and his list grew longer and longer. By the time Amber came over and sat down next to him, he'd started to separate out all the calls by seriousness and area.

She looked down at the lists and charts he had spread across the table. "Wow. You're really keeping on top of this. How many teams do we have?"

"Probably less than we actually need." He didn't mean his answer to seem quite so brusque.

Amber shot him a strange sideways glance. "Do you know how many staff we have, and how many transportation vehicles?"

He glanced over at Ron, trying to hide his frustration. "Ron hasn't told me yet. Search and Rescue say no one leaves unless they deem it necessary. There can be risks of flash flooding."

Ron appeared next to Jack and blanched when he saw the list and map covered in colored dots.

Jack stood up. "The eye of the hurricane has passed. How about we send staff back down to the first floor to reopen the ER? It's important that people have a central point to come to."

Ron nodded in agreement.

"Makes sense." Amber pulled a crumpled piece of paper from her pocket and smoothed it out in front of her. "So, do any of the areas where teams will be sent have patients we'll be looking for?"

He could tell she was trying to sound reasonable. He knew perfectly well that as soon as the winds died down she wanted to find a car and get around all the contacts immediately.

He pulled out his own list. He hadn't forgotten that he'd offered to help her. "Trouble is, it's so dark out there now. With all the debris, the roads will be hard enough to maneuver along. What with no street lighting, things will be much worse." He pointed to colored dots he'd stuck on the map. "The blue dots are addresses where we need to give people antibiotics. What complicates things is that some of these people might not have stayed in their own homes. The statewide evacuation shelters are all based in high schools or elementary schools. Chances are, some of them might have gone there."

"We have no way of telling?"

Jack shook his head. "Not right now. There could be thousands of people in each of the evacuation shelters. With limited communications, there's no way for us to find out."

"Any news about Aaron's parents?"

Jack shook his head again. "I've not heard a thing about them. If I do, I'll let you know."

He could see her swallowing nervously as she pointed to another part of her notes. "These people, there's fourteen of them. That includes the three close contacts who had traveled internationally. We've contacted Florida, Texas and New Zealand. It's up to their own public health departments to make contact and issue the antibiotics. We also had four kids go back to Oahu. Honolulu staff are coordinating for them. Another two kids are on Maui and one more on Kauai. Local doctors will deal with them."

"So that leaves us the kids and staff from the Big Island. How many do we need to still track down?"

"Four. That's not too many. Hopefully we can

coordinate with any team that's going out." She was toying with a strand of her hair. It must be a nerves thing. But it made him feel instantly protective.

"We still have the other six teenagers that were still staying at the surf school. Ty hasn't been able to get hold of anyone else, but he's pretty sure they'll have been evacuated to the Deltarix High School. Six close contacts in one trip. That should make things a bit easier."

Amber bit her bottom lip. She looked over at the map. "So the red dots are the reports of damage or destruction, and the blue dots are the places we still need to go for contact tracing?"

"Yellow are the people that need to be checked on. That doesn't necessarily need to be medical personnel, but since that information is being passed between agencies, I thought it wise to keep it up there." He sighed. "We still have no idea if there's a threat of flooding, or what the roads will be like."

Ron pointed to a part to the north of the city. "During the last tropical storms, these roads were impassable between mudslides and flood damage."

There was a blue dot very close to that area. Jack leaned forward. "Where's the nearest evacuation center to there? Maybe because of what's happened in the past, the residents will have evacuated anyway?"

The radio next to Jack crackled and he picked it up. "Reports of major incident at Deltarix High School."

Amber glanced at the list on the wall and her face paled. "That's one of the evacuation centers. The one we were just talking about."

Jack's pen was poised. "Can you give us some more information?"

"Roof's been torn from the high-school gymnasium where hundreds of the evacuees were waiting out the storm. Reports of serious injuries and multiple minor injuries."

Jack glanced over toward Ron. He waved his hand to attract his attention. "Do you have any idea of numbers?"

The voice crackled at the end of the radio message. "Around six serious. Two head injuries, three with chest injuries or breathing difficulties and another with multiple fractures. Also a number of children with fractures, and another child reported to be seizing."

Jack ran his fingers through his hair and looked at Ron. "It's time. We've got to load up and get out there." He didn't want to be at the end of a radio, manning a desk. He'd never been that type of guy. He'd been asked to triage. Well, the time for triage was over. It was time to get out on the ground and use the skills that he'd been trained in.

Right now he wasn't afraid of the hurricane. Right now he was afraid that people would die if they couldn't get the medical attention they needed—people like Jill.

And no matter what, he couldn't let that happen.

He was trying so hard to give Ron his place. He handed the lists he'd made to him. Jack had been watching the staff in the department for the last two hours and could guess exactly who'd be sent on the teams. "How about you call everyone together and let them know?"

It was the first time since she'd got here that Amber's head had really cleared. She'd stopped thinking about Aaron's parents. Her brain had already worked overtime on that one, imagining a million different ways they could have been injured trying to get to their son. She hated the way her stomach churned over and over. The logical part of her brain just couldn't override the emotional part.

She had patients to seek out—people who were at risk of developing meningitis. And she had other patients to help. Cleaning and stitching had almost felt therapeutic. Getting back to basics. She'd even reviewed a few elderly patients on the medical ward who had taken a downward turn in the last few hours. She was almost sure one had a chest infection and the other a urinary tract infection. Because of the hurricane, X-rays and lab tests would likely be delayed, so she'd ordered antibiotics and IV fluids for them both.

She'd felt useful. She'd felt part of something. And it had sparked something inside her. Which was why she'd finally found the courage to sit down next to the guy who had sparked something else inside her earlier.

Now was not the time to get freaked out. Now

was not the time to worry about someone breaching her inner shell.

There was too much else to worry about. There was too much else happening. She wanted to move back into the tough and sassy woman he'd met at the bar last night. Was that really only twenty-four hours ago?

Jack grabbed some tape and put up the map on the closest wall. He started moving sticky notes around at lightning speed. Ron was at his shoulder.

"We definitely need a team at the high school. There are twenty known casualties, with probably more." Jack looked over his shoulder at the melee of staff. "Another team here." He pointed at a care home. "We know that seven elderly residents were unable to be evacuated along with three members of staff. Red Cross have reports of injuries of a group of tourists on a bus tour."

There was a flash of frustration across Ron's face. "Why on earth didn't they take shelter as instructed?"

"The radio on the bus wasn't working, they didn't hear the alerts, and once the driver realized there was a storm, he pulled over to the side of the road. That bus has overturned just outside Kona."

Ron threw his hands up. "Well, too late now. Any more information on the numbers?"

Jack shook his head. "No. The mobile masts must have gone down just after it was called in. Apparently the caller was given standard advice about sheltering, but there wasn't time for anything else."

Ron had his hands on his hips as he shook his head. "The tour buses are pretty standard—usually single-deckers with around fifty passengers." He ran his fingers across the map, paying attention to the notes Jack had given him and then looking back among his staff and nodding. Jack pressed his lips together. It was hard not to try and take charge. His army ranking meant he was usually the one in charge of any emergency planning.

It was almost as if Ron sensed his thoughts as he gave Jack a sideways glance. "Okay, army doc. Which team do you want to lead?" Jack felt Amber flinch next to him. He knew that her eyes were currently fixed on the blue dots on the map, while her brain did the countdown in hours. The residential home was closest to a few addresses they had to visit, but the nearest evacuation center could also house some of their close contacts. No matter the temptation, he kept his mouth closed.

He wasn't the boss. This time he was only here to assist. He didn't know the area and he didn't know the skills of the staff. This was Ron's team. Not his. He turned to face Ron. "I'll go wherever you need me. Just let me know how I can help."

There was a glimmer of amusement on Ron's face—almost as if he knew Jack was trying to resist interfering.

Ron glanced around, whistled and then put his hands about his head, clapping loudly. "Right, everyone—pay attention. We have work to do, so listen up, people. Okay, Marie Frank, Akito, Sarah, Leia and Tom, I want you all back in the ER with the doors open to receive casualties as soon as we have the all clear. Abram, Jess, Sito and Amal, you'll be team one." He pointed to a position on the map. "I want you out here. Collect your emergency kits. There's an overturned bus with an unknown amount of casualties. Coordinate with the Red Cross. They gave us the initial information. They may also have some staff that can assist."

He turned to face Jack and held his hand above his head. "People, some of you might have already met this guy. This is Jack Campbell, an army doc from Scotland who has offered to assist at this time. In an emergency, we take all the international help we can get. Follow his instructions as you would mine."

He turned toward Amber. "And this is Dr. Amber Berkeley from the Disease Prevention Agency. We have two teenagers in the basement with a strain of meningitis W. Before the hurricane, Dr. Berkeley identified a number of key contacts who require antibiotics. At the moment we only have a rough idea of where those people might be. Dr. Berkeley will give you a list of names and addresses, and some spare antibiotics. If you come across any of these people at evacuation centers, or you are near to the addresses and it's safe, feel free to try and make contact. In the meantime—" his pale gray eyes turned to Amber "—Dr. Berkeley will also be assisting in the field."

Ron pointed to two other members of staff.

"Dr. Campbell will be leading team two along with Dr. Berkeley and Lana and Jamal. Guys, show our new doctors where they can pick up supplies and radios. You guys will be covering the high school where the roof has been damaged. Team three."

He pointed to some other staff and shouted names. "You'll be covering the elderly care center, and also check on the additional needs facility nearby. After that, head to the high school with team two." Ron stopped and took a deep breath. "As soon as we get radio confirmation it's safe to go outside, the police will be here to assist us. Chances are, none of us are going to get any sleep anytime soon. Stay safe, people. Now, let's do what we're trained to."

Amber hadn't even realized she was holding her breath as Ron spoke. It was almost as if he flicked a switch. The buzz began immediately. But instead of more bedlam, it was like a weird kind of organized chaos.

She'd recognized something in Jack during Ron's talk. She could see how hard he found it to defer to someone else. How had that really worked for a guy in the army? An army was all about rank and discipline.

But she'd seen him swallow and tell Ron that he'd go wherever he was needed. Ron must have recognized the struggle too, because he'd almost laughed out loud, then decided they should go to one of the most challenging areas.

It was clear he had faith in the skills of an army surgeon.

But would he have the same kind of faith in her? Her stomach twisted. That awful feeling of having to prove herself all over again.

"Let's go," said Jack. He was already following the two staff they'd been assigned to work with. Amber gave herself a shake and pushed everything else from her head. They followed Lana and Jamal tentatively down the stairs, and after a quick check through the doors, they braced themselves against the continuing wind sweeping through the building and headed toward the ER.

All the staff who arrived in the ER moved seamlessly, locating emergency packs and handing out tabards for all staff. Amber found herself wearing a bright orange vest over her jacket with the word "DOCTOR" emblazoned across it in fluorescent white letters.

It was odd. She'd thought she might feel more awkward than she did. But she seemed to find her place and slot into it. Maybe it was the complete air of calm around Jack. Or the sideways glances he kept shooting at her when he thought she wasn't watching. She tried to keep her professional face in place. There was so much going around about her, it was easy to follow every instruction given and pay attention to the briefings about equipment they could carry, potential patients and what they might face outside.

Lana and Jamal seemed confident in their roles. Lana showed Amber where everything was in her pack and handed her an emergency supply of drugs. They'd moved down to the ER and other staff ensured the department was ready to open. The wind was still fierce outside but the intensity had started to diminish. Eventually, they heard a set of sirens outside. Jack appeared at her shoulder, stuffing something in the bag on her back. She tried to turn around. "Wh…what?" she asked.

"Extra pads," he said casually. Somehow the

sense of him beside her was reassuring. It didn't stop her head going to the place it wanted to be—finding a way to the patients she was supposed to see. Finding out where Aaron's parents were. Keeping to her mission.

Amber was nervous. She couldn't help it. What she really wanted to do was find a working phone and contact the DPA to see if someone else could coordinate information on her patients. Jack seemed a little distant. He did things automatically, almost without any thought. He'd seemed so passionate about his work, it was weird to see him behaving in this oddly detached way. What was it like to do things on automatic pilot?

And her stomach was still twisting in knots about Aaron's parents. Information seemed a bit chaotic right now. She so wished she'd had a chance to talk to them. Maybe she could have persuaded them to stay at home until after the storm. Her gut told her that most parents would have got behind the wheel of a car if their child was at risk, but somehow it just made her feel worse. She hadn't even had the opportunity to try and stop them. That was the thing that frustrated her the most.

The bright orange pack on her back wasn't light. It was jam-packed with just about everything she could need. Her hand still held a copy of the list of patients they hoped to find. As she heard the sound of sirens outside, her heart gave a little lurch. She stepped back over to a desk and picked up an internal phone. "May I?"

The nurse at the desk gave a nod and she quickly dialed the room downstairs. "It's Amber. We're just about to leave. How are Zane and Aaron?"

The nurse gave her a quick rundown. "Holding steady" seemed to be the most appropriate phrase. One minute later the doors were pulled open and some of the Fire and EMS personnel came in. All were wearing heavy gear, helmets and visors. They started handing out similar headwear to the emergency teams. One of the guys shook hands with Ron and had a quick conversation. He turned to face the waiting teams.

"Okay, people. Remember, hazards will be encountered after a hurricane. Live wires, gas leaks, building fires, unsafe structures, flooding, hazardous materials, victims of the trauma and displaced animals. No one travels alone. Everyone keeps in radio contact. If the wind speeds increase again above fifty miles an hour, you'll all be told to stand down until it's safe. All of my staff have flood maps. Listen to what they tell you. Areas may look safe but the ground under the water may be unstable. All our mobile masts are down. Several of our utilities are down. The rainfall is still heavy. Be safe out there, people."

As soon as the fire chief had finished, several of the EMS staff came forward. "Team one, over there. Team two, you're with me. Team three, let's go."

The first things that struck Amber were the wind, the noise and the driving rain. Even though the eye of the hurricane had passed, the weather was still a force to be reckoned with. It wasn't an ordinary ambulance that sat outside. This vehicle looked more like an army vehicle. It still had emergency markings, but also had bigger, thicker tires and an overall heavier build.

They climbed inside and Jack checked over the map with the driver. "Dave," he said as he glanced around at the team. "Consider me your scout. We aren't sure of all the roads as we've only come from the emergency center. It's a few miles to the school, so be prepared."

The radio was fixed to the dashboard with the channel open so they could hear any updates.

Amber stared out of the windows as the vehicle started to slowly move. Some of the trees looked permanently bent in the wind. Some shop fronts with shutters appeared undamaged. Others weren't quite so lucky with gaping holes in the front of their stores. Most of the high-rise buildings they passed were eerily quiet. The city center had plenty of offices that should have been safely evacuated. Some of those windows had obviously been hit by flying debris too, and a few curtains were buffeting in the winds from high floors.

The streets were littered with random and sometimes odd items. Signage, chairs, a table, kitchen utensils and lots of city trash cans rolled around. A few cars were turned on their sides. The wind continued to sideswipe them, but Dave held the vehicle steady. "It's like a disaster movie," breathed Amber.

"Except it's real life," answered Jack, his voice gravelly.

She could hear it. The edge of wariness in his body. He was perched on the edge of the seat, looking constantly from side to side, as if he were waiting for something to jump out at them. It unnerved her. Inside the hospital they'd been relatively safe. Out here? Anything could happen. And even though there were parts of Jack that reminded her of her father, right now she was glad he was at her side.

They turned the next corner. "Darn it!" yelled Dave, and the vehicle came to a screeching halt. They hadn't even been going fast, but Amber found herself flung forward, despite being strapped in.

Part of a building lay in front of them. It was as if the edge of the latest block of apartments had disintegrated onto the road. She looked up and couldn't help but gasp. She could see inside the second-floor sitting room. Pictures were on the wall. There was a door leading…somewhere. Half of a settee was still sitting in the room. But then? Then a whole corner of the room had just disintegrated over the road. "How on earth did that happen?"

Dave very slowly edged the vehicle around the

rubble, mounting the pavement on the other side of the street, continuing to stare upward. "Has to be the roof," he murmured. "Part of it looks torn off, part of it has collapsed downward, taking the edge of the building with it."

Jack shook his head as he adjusted the backpack at his feet. "This hasn't been called in. There could be people in that building."

Amber blinked and looked at the debris on the road. It all just seemed like a pile of bricks, along with an upturned armchair, lampshade and parts of a window. Thankfully, she couldn't see anyone among the rubble. But Jack already had his hand on the door handle.

"I'm going to check the building," he muttered to Dave. "Radio in. The entranceway and stairwell look safe. I'll run up and have a shout, check there's no one stuck inside."

Amber's first thought was to say no. But Dave nodded and Jack was out of the car before she could object. He stuck his head back in the door. "Wait here, you lot. I'll only be five minutes."

"Wait. That can't be a good idea. Should he be going in there?"

Dave shook his head with a half smile. "Nope. But we shouldn't go in any building without a health and safety check after a hurricane. Do you honestly think that's going to happen any-time soon? They're sending us to a high school with half the roof ripped off."

The irony struck her hard. Of course they were. This was always going to be dangerous. Dave radioed in about the damaged building and partially blocked road, while the rest of them stared out of the vehicle windows, waiting for any sign.

A few minutes later Jack appeared with a bun-dle in his arms. Amber couldn't help it. She was out of the vehicle immediately, Lana and Jamal not far behind her.

"It's okay," said Jack as he strode toward them in the strong winds. The elderly woman was huddled in toward his chest. "This is Mary," he said as he placed her inside. "She was sheltering in the stairwell. No serious injuries, just some cuts and bruises. And a whole lot of shock since she was in her sitting room as it collapsed." He gently sat her down and put his hand at the side of her face. "It's okay, Mary. You're safe now."

There was something so caring and tender about the way he spoke to her. It tugged at Amber's heart. What was it about this guy? One second he reminded her of her father and she wanted to sprint into the distance; next second he did something like that and it just melted her heart.

He looked up for the briefest of seconds and his dark brown eyes met hers. He didn't say anything. He didn't have to. Whatever the weird connection between them, it was obvious he felt it too.

After a second he broke their gaze and nodded to Dave. "Nothing serious. We can go on to the high school and tend to her there with the others."

Amber settled in the back with Mary as they set off again. Jamal patched the few small wounds Mary had on her legs and arms, then bundled her under his arm and held her tight, talking to her the whole time.

It was clear she was shocked. Her voice was shaking and tired. She'd missed the transport to the evacuation center and decided to lock down in her house until the hurricane passed. Amber's stomach turned over. Where would Mary go after the storm? Where would anyone go whose house had been damaged?

Fifteen minutes later they reached the high-school evacuation center. Half the roof was missing from the auditorium and gymnasium. Debris was strewn across the football field. There was another emergency vehicle outside, so the team piled out and headed to the main entrance of the school.

Someone with an orange tabard was waiting for them. "Are you the team from Lahuna State Hospital?"

Jack nodded and held out his hand. "Jack Campbell." He nodded over his shoulder toward the rest of them. "Amber, Lana, Jamal and Dave. We've also picked up a woman with a few minor injuries." There was no need for more formal introductions as they all had tabards too with their designation.

The woman put her hand on her chest. She looked as if she might cry. "I'm Chrissie. We have a number of injured people and a whole lot more to assess." She pointed toward one of the classrooms. "Your lady can go in here. We have a few volunteers."

"Take us to the people that are injured," said Jack.

"Wait," said Amber quickly. She handed a note to Chrissie. "Do you have a register of the people here?"

Chrissie looked confused. "We tried to do that, but things got a bit chaotic."

She squeezed Chrissie's hand with the list in it. "Please, can you check these names? It's really, really important we get in touch with these people."

Chrissie stared down at the list in her hand. "I'll do my best."

Amber followed Jack further into the building.

There were a few firefighters already in the building. They were moving debris and assessing damage. One of them shook his head as they approached. "We have a few power issues. Electrical faults. We've put tape over some of the doorways so no one goes inside."

Jack nodded and headed into the main gymnasium. Rain was thudding down onto the floor on the half where the ceiling was missing. Everyone still inside had been moved to the other side. There were a number of people lying on the floor.

Jack shrugged his pack from his shoulder and walked over, setting it down on the floor next to one of the injured. "You over there." He pointed to Amber, then turned to Jamal and Lana. "One over there, and one over there. Let me know what you've got."

Amber took a deep breath as she approached the young woman lying on the floor ahead of her. The woman looked around the same age as herself but her arm was lying at an awkward angle and she had a gash on her head.

Amber knelt down next to her, reaching in her pack for some supplies. "I'm Amber. I'm one of the doctors. What's your name?"

"Kel," she breathed.

Amber tried to do a quick assessment of the patient, pulling a small flashlight from her pack and checking her neuro obs. The woman gave a little groan and her eyelids fluttered open for a second. She attempted to move then let out a yelp. Her arm was obviously broken. Amber grabbed a dressing and covered the wound on the woman's forehead after she'd checked it. The arm was going to take a bit more than a wound dressing.

"When was the last time I dealt with broken bones?" whispered Amber to herself. She touched the woman's other shoulder. "I'm going to give you an injection for the pain," she said lowly, "before I try and move your arm." It only took a matter of seconds to draw up the injection. Amber kept talking to the woman the whole time. She gave her the injection and waited a few minutes for it to take effect. She found a sling in among her supplies. Once the woman's pain was under control, she very gently put the injured arm in a sling.

Where was Jack? She couldn't see him and there were a number of other patients to deal with. Jamal and Lana were dealing with patients of their own, checking wounds and patching dressings. Amber moved on to the next patient. Then the next, then the next. It seemed that lots of people in the evacuation center had been injured, some before the storm, some on the way to the center and some as a result of the roof being ripped off.

Eventually one of the firefighters came to her side. "Dr. Jack said to come and find you. He needs a hand, and wants a rundown on your patients."

A hand she could do. But should she be offended he wanted a rundown on her patients? She asked one of the volunteers to keep an eye on a few people and followed the firefighter outside, then followed him down a corridor into a back entrance of the damaged gymnasium.

There were a few people who looked as if they were standing guard outside one of the doors. "What is it?" she asked.

"The school janitor. He was already injured trying to help someone. Now we think he's been electrocuted."

Amber gulped. Water had seeped into every part of this building due to the roof damage and storm. One of the firefighters handed her a pair of rubber boots. "Put these on before you go any further."

She threw her shoes to the side and pulled on the rubber boots, nodding to the firefighter once she was ready.

But when he opened up the door, she realized she was anything but ready.

Jack was almost hanging from the ceiling, above a floor covered in a few inches of water, and holding on to a man who was trapped in twisted bleachers. He had a plastic portable gurney in two bits next to him.

"Great," he said once he saw her. "Amber, can you bring an airway? I need you to maintain this guy's airway for me." His hands appeared to be on the patient. "But don't touch the floor. You'll need to climb around, across those bleachers. Get a pair of gloves from somewhere."

She tried to make sense of the room. The bleachers were twisted into an almost unrecognizable state. One of the large ceiling lights had landed in the pool of water on the floor. The firefighter next to her spoke into her ear. "The janitor pulled a kid out of here just before that light landed on the floor. He was flung up onto the bleachers with the shock. He's been groaning ever since." The firefighter nudged her. "Your Dr. Jack is quite the gymnast. He managed to make it over there better than some of our boys."

Amber was trying to plot her course along the

edge of the water-lined floor then up toward the tangled bleachers. After a few seconds, she gave a nod. "Okay, I think I can do it." The firefighter handed her some gloves.

"Wait," she asked. "What's Jack going to do while I hold the airway?"

The firefighter pressed his lips together. "Oh, he's also trying to stop the bleeding."

"What bleeding?"

She looked back at the floor again and directly under the bleachers to where Jack and the patient were. The water was stained with red. This guy was bleeding heavily. However he'd landed on those bleachers, it hadn't been pretty.

She shook her head. "Don't worry. I get it."

It was obvious that Jack couldn't take his other hand from wherever the wound site was. She bent down and pulled one of his wound pads from her pack and stuffed it inside her jacket. It took a few moments to maneuver her way around the edge, taking care to avoid any hint of water, to where one of the firefighters was waiting to give her a punt up onto the bleachers.

"Ready?" he asked.

"As I'll ever be," she replied. Her hands caught

on to a plastic chair and she moved from one to another, ducking between them and squeezing her body from side to side.

"Any word from the power company?" shouted Jack. "If we could be sure the power was off, things would be a whole lot easier."

"Can't even get through," replied one of the firefighters. "Ironic, really. The one place we actually want a power cut is the place we can't get it."

Another guy came up alongside him and shouted over to Jack. "We've looked for the breakers but we think the box has been covered by the debris from the roof."

Jack pulled a face as Amber continued to thread her way through the twisted bleachers. The last part was the toughest; she had to shrug off her jacket and push it through first before she could squeeze through the small space, finally ending up breathless next to Jack.

"How on earth did you get the plastic gurney up here?"

Jack raised his eyebrows. "It's plastic. We just threw it across the floor then had to work out a way to pick it up on this side without getting shocked." He gestured to the large plastic pole next to him and a thick pair of rubber gloves. As she looked down at them she caught sight of the blood on Jack's clothes.

"Are you okay?" she asked, instantly worried.

"It's not mine," he replied quickly. His jaw was tense with a little tic at the side, as if his muscles were straining. One hand was positioned at the patient's head and neck, keeping his airway propped open, the other pressed hard against the patient's side.

Something flickered in her brain. "Wait," she said quickly as she unfolded her jacket. "I brought one of your wound pads."

His eyes lit up. "Great. Thanks." He rolled his eyes. "I left my pack behind when I came in here. We thought he'd just been shocked. I didn't realize there were other injuries." She opened the wound pad and held it toward him. He grabbed it and replaced it with the one he'd been using. As he pulled it upward Amber could see that the traditional dressing had virtually disintegrated.

"Let me help," she said as she moved her position to near the head of the trolley. She pulled an airway from her pocket and worked around

Jack, inserting it into the janitor's mouth. Once she was sure it was safely in position, she placed her hands carefully on either side of the janitor's head, her fingers covering Jack's. He looked up and met her gaze.

"You got it?" he asked.

There was something about his words and the expression in his gaze. All the way along she'd felt as if his natural position was to take over everything. To take charge. But now Jack was the one asking for help.

She'd thought she'd have to ask him a million questions out here—out of her comfort zone. But he hadn't been around and she'd coped fine. Maybe the director at the DPA was right— maybe she was ready for more field missions.

"I've got you," she whispered in reply.

In that second she felt a wave. A connection. An understanding of the overwhelming pain in his eyes. A deep, fathomless hurt that he never revealed or let bubble to the surface. Jack Campbell never asked for help. He never counted on anyone else. He was solitary in his life. For reasons that she couldn't even begin to imagine. It was the first depth, the first exposure she'd seen from him, and it was the truest thing she had ever felt.

Even though she'd only just got to know him, she got the overwhelming impression that he'd have her back. A warm feeling flowed through her, filling her with the confidence that she sometimes lacked. This strong, fearless army surgeon needed her help and she was happy to give it. Always. And something about it felt good. Special.

He released his hand, pulling it gently out from under her firm grip. For a second the tension left his shoulders, but a few seconds later he put his second hand down with his first on the wound.

"What's he done?" asked Amber. The sky was dark above and there were no artificial lights. From this position she couldn't really make out what was wrong.

"He's been pierced by a bit of the bleachers. From the amount of blood, I think he might have damaged his spleen."

She licked her lips. "How's your wound pad doing?"

Jack gave a brief nod of his head. He lifted one hand from the wound site. The glove he was wearing wasn't smeared in blood this time. It was more or less wiped clean. He put it back down. "I think things are clotting. The blood loss has certainly slowed. Before it just seemed like a steady flow. Nothing I was using was stemming the blood flow."

She gave an appreciative nod. "That's another life, Jack. Another life saved."

She shifted a little. Her position was awkward, her legs spread across an unstable base above the still-wet floor, her back starting to ache already. The space across the floor was vast, with easy access to the door if only there weren't a chance of water filled with electricity in their way.

"Jack, how are we going to get out of here? We might be able to clamp this gurney around him but there's no way we can fit it through the spaces we climbed through." She wrinkled her nose and stared down at the floor. "The gurney is plastic. Could we lower it to the floor and push him across again?"

Jack raised his eyebrows. "You want to take that chance?"

She pulled a face. "Not really."

"Me either."

She stared at the rope around his waist, looped around something hanging from part of the ceiling and allowing him to slightly change position as needed. "How on earth did you do that?"

He grinned. "One of the firefighters is some kind of mountaineer. At first they were worried I shouldn't actually touch the bleachers. They rigged the rope and tied it to me before I set off. Theory was it would keep me off the floor if everything else around me collapsed."

She stared down at her waist and raised her eyebrows. "Great. Where's mine?"

He nodded toward her feet. "You got the rubber boots. That's your insurance policy." He wiggled one foot at her. "I'm still on the regular army boots. Not quite the same."

She noticed he was still keeping his hands firmly down at the janitor's wound. She watched carefully the rise and fall of the janitor's chest. At least he was maintaining his airway, without any oxygen. That was good. Even if he had suffered some kind of electric shock, he was still breathing. If only she had a spare hand right now to reach for his pulse.

"Any idea about his cardiac situation right now?"

"I'd love to know about his cardiac situation. But I've run out of hands. You have too. Let's just say, due to the amount of blood loss, we know his heart has kept beating. I just wish he'd regain consciousness so I could try and assess him."

Amber shook her head. "With that wound, I'm not sure you do. How much pain will he be in? I don't know how still he would stay and we're not in the most stable of positions."

Jack gave a reassuring nod. "I know that." For a second his dark eyes twinkled. "Did you ever imagine when you met the jet-lagged Scotsman in the bar we'd end up working together in the middle of a hurricane?"

She let out a quiet laugh and shook her head. "If you'd asked me to place bets that night, I'm pretty sure this would never even have been on my radar."

"Still annoyed I didn't tell you I was a doctor?"

"Till my dying day." She laughed.

Jack's face changed. There was the briefest flash of something and Amber's insides flip-flopped, cringing. She'd said the wrong thing—but she had no idea why.

"Dr. Jack!" came the shout behind her.

She wanted to swivel around but her position made it awkward. Jack replied for them both. "We're almost ready."

"What are they doing?" asked Amber as she tried to see out of the corner of her eye.

"It's the backup plan," said Jack. "Just think really big planks of wood."

There were loud noises behind her. Scraping, thudding and the odd splash of water. She could also hear quite a lot of groans and moans behind her as the firefighters positioned the planks of wood.

After what seemed like forever, there was a voice not too far behind her. "Okay, Docs, we think we're just about ready. The wood is in place. We're on it. We're going to come toward you and help you clamp that gurney into place. Then we'll try and bring you all down together. Whatever you do, as you come down from the bleachers, make sure you step directly onto the wood. We're still not sure about the state of the electrics and the main floor is still wet. No-body touches the floor. Are we clear?"

Jack glanced at her. "We're clear," he shouted back.

But the firefighter didn't seem to be happy with that response. "Dr. Berkeley, did you get that? I need to know you understand before any-one moves."

Amber shouted back. "Okay, I've got it. Just let me know when."

From that point, Jack was her eyes. He told her where everyone was, and how soon it was until they were at her back. And they were a good partnership. She held her hands steady, support-ing the janitor's airway, even though they felt as though they could cramp. It was the longest time until she felt a pair of large hands at her waist. It made her start a little. "Right behind you, Doc," came the deep voice at her back. "I'm going to come around your side and grab one side of the gurney."

She felt his large body brush against hers as the firefighter came around her side, squeezing his body next to one side of the gurney. Another guy appeared at the other side and they coordinated with Jack and Amber.

"We'll take the weight of the gurney. Your job is to keep doing whatever it is you need to do. We're going to move slow and steady. Let us know if there's an issue. Dr. Berkeley, we know you're going to be walking backward. We're going to have someone else behind you to guide you, and make sure you don't step off the planks."

It was the first time she actually felt a bit nervous. Of course. Stepping off the planks could result in a nasty shock. Jack met her gaze again. "Okay?"

"Okay," she replied, her voice a little shakier than she'd like. She really wanted to move her hands, just for a second, just to stretch them to stop the cramp setting in. Last thing she wanted was her hands to spasm when she was holding this airway.

She took a few breaths and concentrated on the rise and fall of the janitor's chest. That was what she needed to focus on. She could do this.

The firefighter to her right started talking

slowly and steadily. "We're going to take the weight on three. Ready? One, two, three."

The gurney lifted just a little under her hands. She felt another pair of hands at her waist and heard the voice of a female firefighter. "Dr. Berkeley, I'm Kate. I'm here to guide you. I want you to take one slow step backward."

It was harder than it should be. She wasn't on a flat surface. She was still halfway up the twisted bleachers. Her hands were already fixed in position. Now she was stepping downward with no weight to steady herself. But the hands at her waist were strong and firmly reassuring. Not only did they feel as though they could take part of her weight, they also felt as if they could keep her straight and steady. She felt her way with one foot, finding another part of the bleachers to stand on. Then she shifted her weight, ready to move the next foot.

The firefighters watched her constantly, as did Jack, the gurney sliding steadily closer toward her. Jack was finding it easier to move; he could put a little weight on the gurney as he found his footing to move. Amber concentrated on the firm hands at her waist and the steadying voice of Kate. When she finally felt her foot reach a thick plank of wood on the floor, she let out a huge sigh.

Kate gave a laugh. "Don't be too relieved," she said. "We've still got a bit to go. And, believe me, these guys couldn't put planks of wood in a straight line if they tried."

Slowly and steadily they moved. Jack's eyes were on hers. He didn't talk. He just kept watching her. In any other set of circumstances she would have been slightly unnerved. But it wasn't like that. It was reassuring.

Once they reached the entranceway and stepped off the wood and onto the normal flooring in the corridor outside, Jamal was waiting with a bag and mask to take her place. He gave her a gentle nudge. "Let me take over for a bit," he said as she stumbled back wearily and stretched out her aching hands.

The gurney was lowered to the ground. Jack moved instantly to the side of the gurney and lifted the edge of his wound pad. Amber couldn't help herself. She had to see too. She knelt on the floor next to him. Lana had appeared too and fixed a BP cuff around the janitor's arm, checking his blood pressure and taking his pulse with her fingers. "Can't beat old-fashioned methods." She winked at Amber.

Amber could see a bead of sweat on Jack's brow. Just how long had he been in position while she'd been dealing with other patients? "Has it worked?" she asked.

Jack gave a relieved breath. "I hope so. It looks as if a clot has formed." He looked at the readings that Lana had taken. "His blood pressure is low. His pulse fast and thready. He's not regained consciousness. He really needs to be back at the hospital."

Amber nodded. "I agree. I've got another patient next door with a broken arm, and a possible head injury. I also patched up a woman with a shoulder injury and another with a whole array of cuts to her face and arms."

Jack sighed. "Before I got called here, I dealt with an older man with a crush injury to his lower leg. Part of the ceiling caught him when it was ripped off. And a woman who sheltered some kids and ended up with a spinal injury." Amber's eyes widened but he shook his head. "She's not paralyzed but she's got a loss of sensation in one of her legs. She needs proper assessment. We've got two kids who had asthma attacks because they forgot their inhalers. We managed to find some and they're stable now. Another kid had a minor seizure but that's stopped and he's come around."

Jamal pulled a list from his pocket. "Here. I collated some details while you two were trying to get electrocuted," he said wickedly. "We radioed in, and they're sending a few extra ambulances in our direction." He looked at Jack. "You just need to decide who goes first."

A list. She'd forgotten. She'd forgotten about her own list.

Jack must have caught the expression on her face, because he raised own eyebrow in silent question. She shook her head and stood up. "You've got this. Let me see if there's anyone else needing to be patched up before the ambulances arrive. I'll let you know if there's anything serious."

She stretched out her back for a few seconds, trying to relieve the ache she was feeling, and made her way back to the main gymnasium. There were a few more staff, helping patch patients up. She found her pack again and emptied its contents on the floor next to her, then made a quick check of Kel and her broken arm, giving her some more pain relief and checking her neuro obs again.

The evacuation center had over two thousand people in it—they were lucky there weren't more seriously injured. Lots of the people in the center volunteered to help and some had first-aid certificates or previous experience in the health service.

Jack appeared at her side. "Have you finished sorting out who goes first?" she asked him.

"We've got fourteen people who need transport to the hospital sometime soon. I found out our janitor is called Hugo. He's going, along with the lady with the spinal injury, a woman with a head injury and the older gentleman with the broken tib and fib. We only have two ambulances initially, so I've had to prioritize."

Amber leaned in a little and looked at the list in his hand. She could see Kel, the woman with the broken arm and head injury, on the second list. On any other day of the week, she would have wanted to get her assessed sooner. But things were different here. She wasn't unconscious. The other patients would actually take priority.

Jack must have noticed her expression. "You don't agree?" He seemed surprised, but held up the list for her to look at. "If you think differently, let me know."

She swallowed. She hadn't expected that. He actually wanted to know if she had other ideas—even though this wasn't her specialist area. Her fingers crumpled around the list in her pocket as she shook her head. "I don't disagree. I understand why you've prioritized them. How much longer until we get ambulances again? I'd like to get Kel checked over in the next round of patients."

He pulled out the radio from his pocket. "The first should arrive in around ten minutes. It could be an hour before they're back."

"Do we stay here?"

Jack gave her a curious stare. "You can't let it go, can you?"

"What?"

He smiled and shook his head. "Don't pretend with me. You're itching to find out about the close contacts of the meningitis, aren't you?"

He handed her the radio. "Here. Call in. Check on Aaron and Zane and see if anyone has recorded seeing any more of the close contacts."

Amber took the radio gratefully. She wanted to find out how many people were still out there without any medicines. She talked into the radio as she walked back toward the entrance point where Chrissie was based. It only took a few minutes to find out that Chrissie had managed to find the group of boys who had come from the surf school. They'd thought there were six, but it turned out to be seven. One of the boys who was supposed to go someplace else had been delayed by the weather and ended up here. Amber signaled to Lana, and she came and helped her talk to the teenagers and distribute the antibiotics.

Jack appeared at her side. "Ambulance is here. We're loading the first patients. How are Zane and Aaron?"

She gave her head the briefest shake. "Good, and not so good. Aaron has picked up. He's started to respond and come round. Zane is still the same. No change. His BP and temp are in normal limits but he's just not woken up yet."

"Has there been disease progression? Septicemia?"

"Thankfully no. But this whole strain worries me. I'd be much happier if I could find the rest of the close contacts."

Jack seemed to stare ahead for a few seconds. Then the edges of his lips seemed to hint upward. "I was going to ask if you wanted to head back to the hospital with the patients, or if you wanted to stay here and treat any more casualties that come in."

She could hear the slight edge in his voice. He was teasing her. Just a little. "Or…?"

He drew himself up and pushed his shoulders back. It was that second—that second that she saw the man who had served in the army and done two tours of duty. The man who had saved lives and had to juggle priorities in a way she probably never would.

He met her gaze with his dark brown eyes. "Or we could volunteer to stay out here. To help at the bus, or elsewhere, and see if we can drop any more of the antibiotics off."

Her heart gave a little leap. He got her. He understood her. She smiled and folded her arms across her chest. "I think I'll take option three."

CHAPTER FIVE

IT WAS DARK. More than dark—with the power cuts throughout the city it was virtually a blackout. It seemed that only sporadic places had power, so parts of the city glowed like little bulbs on a Christmas tree. Total wrong time of year.

It made Jack catch his breath. Dave, their driver, had helped take people back to the hospital and they'd coordinated with Ron in ER and managed to visit a few of the addresses in the surrounding area where close contacts resided, along with a few other addresses where they'd been asked to check on vulnerable adults.

They decided to go back to the evacuation center and help as best they could. The school kitchens had been opened and manned by a whole host of volunteers. Chrissie pressed some food into their hands and pointed them down a corridor. "We're short of space. But you'll find somewhere down there to sit down for the night."

Amber looked down as her stomach growled loudly. Her hair was pulled back from her face in a haphazard way and there were tired lines around her eyes, but somehow they still had a little sparkle. "Oops. I'd forgotten how hungry I was. It's been a crazy day." She leaned her head against his shoulder.

Jack paused in the corridor; he couldn't help it. "I feel like we should go back to the hospital in case there are other patients to see."

She lifted her head back up. "Jack. Take a breath. We've been working all day, and if we have to pull a night shift, then we will. But let's just sit down for five minutes."

He took a deep breath. That angsty feeling that had been in his stomach all day was still there. It was constantly there. He'd just learned to live with it. Learned to live with the fact he was always looking over his shoulder, waiting for the unexpected.

Every part of his body wanted to keep living on the adrenaline. To keep going, to find the next person to help. But the truth was, his muscles ached. The aroma coming from the food in his hand was tempting. And the thought of sitting down for five minutes didn't seem quite so alien as it might have. Particularly when he was with Amber.

He nodded. "Okay, then—you win. But five minutes. There's probably still a whole host of people that need help. The damage from the hurricane seems huge."

He followed Amber down the corridor. Every room they reached seemed packed with people, some sitting, some lying on the floor. Amber frowned as they struggled to find somewhere to sit.

Suddenly Jack had a brain wave as they kept walking. He bent toward her ear. "I have an idea. Back this way, I think."

Two minutes later he found what he was looking for. The janitor's storeroom. He nudged the handle with his elbow to open the door. Sure enough, it was empty, even though it was tiny. There was a metal cage packed with supplies. A large chair in one corner and a mop and bucket in the other. Amber turned toward him. "Good call. Now let's sit down."

He thought about being polite for a second,

then realized they were past that point, so he let her sit down first, then crushed in next to her.

She laughed as he joined her, giving him a last glimpse of those bright blue eyes as the door slowly closed behind them.

"Oops," giggled Amber as they sat in the pitch darkness. "I guess there's no light in the store cupboard."

"I guess not," agreed Jack. "Looks like we might need to eat in the dark."

"I can do that. I can eat anywhere. I'm so hungry," said Amber.

Within a few minutes their eyes started to adjust to the darkness, the only light being the thin strip at the bottom of the door from the corridor outside.

Amber finished eating and set her paper plate on the floor, sagging back into the chair. Jack finished too and clashed shoulders as he rested back beside her.

"Do you think this is really a chair for one?"

"I don't care." Amber waved her hand. "After the day we've had, I'm happy to share. Hey, do you think we should have gone back to the hotel?"

Jack shook his head. "I was wondering though—we weren't the only doctors at the conference. There were lots of others. I wonder if anyone has thought to draft them in to help."

Amber sighed. "Please tell me that in an emergency situation, some of them will have volunteered like we have. It can't possibly just be us."

She stretched out her arms in front of her, then clasped her hands to stretch out her fingers too.

"Are you stiff? Sore?" It suddenly struck him that he'd asked Amber to do things today that were totally out of her comfort zone. When was the last time she'd had to support an airway? And she'd done it expertly—just like checking broken bones and assessing a potential head injury.

"I'm just trying to stretch out the sore bits," she confessed. "I thought my hands were going to cramp at one point when I was supporting the airway." She shook her head. "And we definitely didn't need that to happen."

Jack smiled at her. "You did well today, Amber. Better than others that I've worked with in the past."

It took her a few seconds to answer. "Thanks…

I think. Truth was, I *was* worried. I thought I might forget everything and have to ask you to remind me. But once I started, everything just kind of fell into place." She let out a sigh. "Maybe the director was right. Maybe I should do more field missions."

"The director?"

"Of the DPA. He's been at me for a while, telling me it's time to do some more field missions."

"I thought you'd already done some."

She nodded slowly. "Oh, I have. But I've always been part of a team. I've always had other medics and nurses around me. I've never actually been the one in charge. I guess I've just been a little afraid."

Now he was curious. He shifted onto one hip so he faced her a little better. "Afraid of what? You're a capable and competent doctor."

Her head dropped and her hands kneaded together in her lap. "Amber?" he pressed.

She let out a long slow breath. "I know I am. I know that I'm capable at what I do. Infectious disease is my comfort zone. I like it—more than that, I enjoy the work. The variety. The locations." Her head lifted and even in the dark he could see her meet his gaze. "But…" Her voice tailed off.

"But what?" He couldn't understand why she would doubt herself.

She leaned her head back against the chair, her eyes staring out in the darkness. "I guess I've spent my life feeling as if I wasn't good enough."

Jack shook his head. "Why on earth would you think that?"

She blinked and he thought he could catch a glimmer of moisture in her eyes. "It was just the life I was brought up with," she said slowly. "My father was obsessed with his work as a surgeon. My mother and I barely saw him. Even when we did, he would spend his time at home, studying journals or taking hospital calls. My mother was basically a widow on the day that she had me. It was never a marriage, and he was never a father."

Jack held his breath at the intensity of her words. He could hear the pain in her voice. The rawness of it all. This obviously ran deep.

He remembered small parts of their original conversation at breakfast. He still couldn't really get his head around it. "Surely, he was proud of the results you got to get into medical school, then the fact you qualified?" He put his hand on his chest. "I don't have kids, and would never want to push them in any direction, but if any of my kids went after their dream and achieved it, I would be over the moon for them. Isn't a parent's job to be proud of their kid?"

Her voice cracked. "Maybe. In an ideal world. Instead, I had a father who never seemed to notice or acknowledge me, or my mother, and now, after he's gone, I feel as if my mom wasted forty years of her life on someone who never loved or appreciated her."

He reached out and took her hand in his. He could tell how upset she was by this. "But she got you. And I bet she's prouder than you can ever imagine. I can't second-guess your parents' relationship, but she probably has a whole host of reasons for why she never left. But now? Now she can pursue whatever she wants, and know that her daughter has her back." He squeezed her hand. "And I'm sorry about your dad. When did he die?"

Amber cleared her throat. "A couple of years ago. It was ironic, really. The surgeon had an aortic aneurysm. He could have been screened at any point, but hadn't found the time."

Jack nodded. He didn't need to ask any questions. As a fellow surgeon, he completely understood how fatal a ruptured aortic aneurysm was.

He couldn't help but try and lighten the mood. "So, runaway bride, are you still dead set against dating doctors?"

It was almost as if something in the air changed between them instantly.

Her voice rose in pitch. "Oh, we're going down that road again, are we?"

"Yeah, well. It seems I've got five minutes on my hands."

"Okay, then. So, I've had a lifetime's experience of an almost vacant father, then a follow-up with the jerk of the century."

Jack gave a little laugh. "Yeah, the guy you left in full tuxedo standing at the end of an aisle."

She gave a smothered laugh too. "Yip. But I did it because he was a butt-licking, using social climber." She turned to face Jack, their faces just a few inches apart. "It seems I have terrible taste in men."

His lips automatically turned upward. He

could smell a hint of her floral scent. It had been there earlier, but after the day they'd had, he would have expected it to vanish. But, as they sat together with their bodies pressed close, he could smell it again. If he reached up right now he could touch her cheek—the way he should have done after he'd met her in the bar. But in a way, it was probably better that he hadn't. At least now he knew why this intriguing, smart, sassy woman wanted to brush him off. And although her exterior was sassy, her interior was entirely different. How many people actually knew that about Amber?

"Hey," she said quietly. "I've spilled a whole lot more than I ever usually do. What're your dark secrets? You've just told me that you've got no kids. Well—none that you know of. But what else don't I know? After all, I have spent the night with you. Will I get messages at some point from a wife, an ex-wife, a girlfriend, and have to reassure them that actually nothing happened between us?"

He sucked in a breath. Even though his eyes had adjusted, they were still in the dark. He could see her profile, her eyes and her eyelashes, all highlighted by the tiny strip of light at the bottom of the door. There was something so private about this—even though they were in an evacuation center with around two thousand other people. They'd found a tiny little spot where they could be alone. And he was grateful for it.

Even though they were in the dark, he closed his eyes. It seemed easier somehow. "I'm single. I've never been married. I don't have an ex-wife."

Even as he said the words out loud, he knew how they sounded. As if he were telling part of a story but not it all.

"But..."

He sucked in another breath. "But then there was Jill."

Amber's voice was a little more high-pitched than normal. "Jill? Who is Jill?"

"Jill was my girlfriend. For just over a year." He let out a wry laugh. "Though she didn't like to be called that. She preferred The Boss."

Amber's voice was wary. It seemed she'd picked up on the fact he was using past tense. "Sounds like someone I would like."

The words struck a chord with him. Jill would have liked Amber. He could imagine them as friends. Jill would certainly have put Amber straight about her choice in men—him included.

"She was good. She was…great." This time it was more difficult to suck in a deep breath. He never really discussed Jill. Not with those who'd served with her, nor with her family after the funeral. It just made everything too real. Too human.

"I was sick. I was operating on a soldier who'd lost his lower limb. It was a tricky op—long—and I started to have abdominal pain. I just ignored it and kept going. By the time I finished I collapsed. My appendix had ruptured."

"What? For crying out loud, Jack, how much pain must you have been in? Wasn't there anyone who could take over from you?"

He winced. "Probably. But the guy on the table was a friend. And he'd already lost so much. I knew how he would feel when he woke up. I also knew that he'd want to get back on his feet. I had to do the best surgery I could to give him a chance of a prosthetic limb. I didn't want him to have to spend the next eighteen months needing revision after revision, when I could take the time to try and get things as good as they could be."

Amber nodded slowly as if she understood. "So what happened next?"

Jack squeezed his eyes closed again. "When I was in surgery…there was a retrieval—when something's gone wrong in the field they sometimes send out a medical team to bring back the injured. It can be the difference between life and death." They were still holding hands, but this time her other hand closed over his, holding it tight, supporting him to continue. "I was always the person that went. Except this time—this time I was in the operating theater on the table. So Jill went. She was an army-trained medic and she was good. As good as any doctor. But they never made it. Their vehicle hit an IED."

Amber didn't hesitate for a second. She pulled her hands away from his and wrapped her arms around his neck, enveloping him in a bear hug and pressing her face next to his. Her breath warmed the skin at the bottom of his neck. "Oh, Jack. I am so, so sorry. That's cruel. I can't even begin to imagine how that feels."

He stayed there. He let her hug him. He let her hug him in a way he'd never really let anyone hug him since it happened. He'd had a few awkward hugs at the funeral from Jill's mom, dad and sister. But he'd only met them on a few occasions briefly. He didn't really know them the way that he'd known Jill.

So it just hadn't felt right. Not when he was so busy building a shell around himself. One that wouldn't let him feel. One that would let him channel all his emotions and energies someplace else.

The sensation gripped him so much it was almost a physical pain. Amber just kept holding him. She didn't let go. And after what seemed like forever, the tension in all his muscles that he permanently held tight finally started to dissipate. He was so conscious of her cheek against his. She didn't seem to mind the fact his bristles must be scraping her skin.

He could feel the heat emanate from her body, and after the fierce winds of the hurricane it was like a warm comfort blanket. Only trouble was, the reaction his body was having was nothing like a warm blanket. It was more like a spontaneous firework.

And his head was trying to work out what was going on around him.

It had happened again. He'd actually *felt* something.

It had happened on the bleachers, when Amber had lifted her head and just stared at him. The connection had been like a punch to the stomach. The way she'd held his gaze, even though they'd been in the middle of something major, and just looked at him. Unflinchingly. As if she'd seen more than was actually there, and buried deep down to find the rest.

He hadn't really wanted to believe it then. He'd been holding his hands against a man's side, trying to stop him bleeding to death. For the last two years his mind had never been anywhere but on the job.

But for the briefest few seconds those big blue eyes had connected with something, tugged at something inside him, in a way he hadn't expected.

Or had he? The last few days had been crazy. He'd been attracted to her as soon as he'd seen her sashaying across the room and slaying potential suitors with a mere look. From her casual, unhindered and sparkly chat in the bar, to her professional, passionate, presenting face she'd shown at the conference. To her dismissal of him at breakfast when she'd found out he was a doctor, to the moment that he'd stepped forward and pressed his head against hers because it had just felt as if she'd needed it.

In every subtle way, he'd found himself drawn to this improbable woman. Someone who, it turned out, had just as many layers as he had.

He didn't even know where to start anymore.

But his body seemed to.

He lifted his hand to her face and touched the side of it gently, pulling back from their hug just enough to give him room to maneuver.

He should ask permission. Because his brain was so muddled he clearly wasn't thinking straight. So he just kept his hand on her soft cheek, tilted her head up toward his and put his lips on hers.

He was hesitant. But Amber wasn't. As soon as he brushed against her lips she ran her fingers through his hair at the back of his head, urging him closer, and her mouth opened to his. What started as tentative and questioning progressed quickly. Amber Berkeley knew how she wanted to be kissed. His hands tangled through her hair, tugging it from the ponytail band. His kisses moved from her lips to her ear and neck, but she was too impatient for that, pulling him to her mouth. She changed position, straddling him on the chair so she was on his lap, letting his hands run up and down the curves of her waist. Her hands moved from his neck to his chest, resting there while they continued to kiss.

There was a noise outside. A shout that permeated the dark world of the storeroom they'd claimed as their own. They both froze and pulled apart, listening to see if the shout would return.

This time it was Amber who pressed her forehead against his. She let out a light laugh. Her breath warmed his skin as she whispered, "Just so you know, I don't date doctors."

He laughed. "Just so you know, I don't kiss on the first date."

She tapped his chest. "This isn't the first date. This is about the third. And anyway, it doesn't matter because—"

"I don't date doctors." He said it simultaneously with her. "Well, that's a relief."

Amber climbed off him as another shout came from outside. "Think we should see what's happening?"

He nodded as he picked their food containers from the floor. "Let's face it. Someone's going to need something from the store cupboard eventually."

He thought for a second she was going to say something else as her hand paused on the door handle, but her head gave the tiniest shake and she pulled it open toward them.

There were more people in the corridor outside, but if anyone wondered what they were doing in the store cupboard, no one mentioned it. Jack walked over to the main entranceway. A number of firefighters and police were gathered there, comparing maps and discussing next steps.

"Give me two minutes," said Amber. "Lana's just given me a wave to check someone over." He nodded as she disappeared.

"Anything I can help with?" Jack asked as he approached the main desk.

"Oh, there you are." Jamal walked up behind them and handed over the radio. "Ron was wanting to talk to you."

Jack turned the dial on the radio and put it to his ear, checking in with Ron. "Where do you need us?"

One of the firefighters turned around as he heard the instructions Jack was given. He waited until Ron was finished then gestured Jack over toward the main table.

"We're getting short of drivers. We can give you a vehicle. But at this point you'll be on your own." He pointed to part of the map. "There's been some flooding around the coastal areas. We're more inland here, but we think there has been around twelve inches of rainfall during the hurricane—and the rain hasn't stopped yet. There's still a chance of flooding from swollen rivers and rain coming off the hills."

The firefighter looked at Jack a little warily. "It might be better to wait until daylight."

"Wait until daylight for what?" asked Amber as she walked back up.

Jack turned to face her. He knew exactly how the words he was about to say would affect her.

"To be part of the search party for Aaron's parents. They've never arrived and are now presumed missing. It's time to go look for them."

CHAPTER SIX

ONE MINUTE SHE was kissing a man she shouldn't; next minute her heart was plummeting into her shoes.

"They haven't appeared?"

Jack shook his head. "Someone has reported a car off the road. It was an ambulance who were resuscitating another patient, so they couldn't stop. But they glimpsed a black car in the trees just outside the city. It's the road they would be expected to be on if they were traveling between Hilo and Kailua Kona."

She gulped. "Then we have to go. We have to go and see if it's them. Even if it isn't them, someone could be hurt." She looked around, trying to remember where she'd left her pack.

"Give me a minute." His voice was authoritative. It was the kind of thing she'd expected earlier from Jack. He walked back over to the table and started talking to one of the firefighters while she scrabbled around locating her jacket and pack. "Lana? Are you coming?"

Lana shook her head. "Can't. Sorry. I've got a sick kid that I'll need to transfer with to the hospital. She's asthmatic and is having problems."

"Anything I can help with?"

Lana shook her head. "I can cope. I should be gone in the next five minutes. But, hey," she said, "I've got another one from your list." She pointed to a name. "This family are here. The younger kids are nephews of Zane and had contact in the last few days. I've given them the antibiotics that they should need."

"Thank you." Amber gave her a relieved hug but Lana wasn't finished.

"Here." She bent down and pulled something from Amber's pack. "I think you should keep this handy. On a night like this, you'll need it."

Amber stared down at the heavy flashlight in her hand. Of course. Exactly what she'd need on a dark roadside. Her heart was starting to beat a bit erratically and she was starting to regret eating that food as her stomach churned.

Jack appeared at her elbow with a different dark jacket in his hand. He was already wearing one with his luminous "DOCTOR" tabards over the top. "Here, one of the firefighters gave me this for you. Apparently the rain is still really heavy and they think we might need it."

She automatically pulled her tabard over her head, shrugged off her own thin jacket and pulled on the thicker, sturdier one with a large hood. "Should I be worried that they've given us this?"

"Let's hope not," replied Jack quickly.

She'd seen him. She'd seen him at his most exposed. She'd held him. She'd kissed him after he'd told her things that could break her heart.

But right now it was almost as if that had never happened. It was almost as if he'd pulled a mask—an invisible shield—into place. Something she'd never been able to do. Everything now seemed so precise. So clinical.

"Where's Dave?" she asked as she slung her backpack over her shoulder.

"We have to drive ourselves. There are too many reports right now to deal with. One of the firefighters has given me directions. The roads were apparently passable a few hours ago. Let's hope they're still the same."

"They've been out there for a few hours?"

Jack held up his hands. "Truth is, I don't know when it was called in. All I know is we've been asked if we can go." He held up the radio. "If we need assistance we let them know. They don't have any spare people to come with us."

Amber shivered. She hated this. Everything about it made her fear the worst. But she tilted her chin and looked Jack in the eye. "Then let's go."

The road leading away from the high school started out relatively debris free. But as they started to wind further out, tree branches and bushes were scattered all around them. Jack drove slowly, taking care around corners. The wind was still strong, buffeting them from side to side, but they only passed one other emergency vehicle on the road. It seemed that everyone else had listened to the instructions to stay inside until they got word it was safe to go back out.

The rain was relentless and Amber was glad of the change of jacket. "I'm going to slow down a bit," Jack said to her. "You watch one side of the road and I'll watch the other. Hopefully we'll come across the car soon."

It was still black outside. They left the city behind and moved out more toward the mountains and green landscape. The few glimmers of light were left far behind them. It was hard trying to scan the dark landscape as they traveled forward. Trees and bushes lined the road. And on a few occasions they stopped at a felled tree, mistaking its dark outline for something else. But eventually their headlights swept over the familiar outline of the back of a car, protruding slightly at the side of the road.

"There!" shouted Amber, her heart rate quickening instantly.

Jack slammed on the brakes and they both jumped out, leaving the engine running and lights facing the foliage.

Amber's heart raced madly as she waded through the foliage on one side, as Jack strode through on the other side.

There were definitely two people in the car. There was condensation on the inside of the windows. The front end of the car had impacted on a large tree trunk and had completely crumpled.

She could see where the airbags inside had deployed then gradually deflated again.

Jack yanked the door open on his side. Amber pulled at the door on her side. It had a large dent in it and wouldn't open. The ground was muddy beneath her feet and she struggled to stay upright as she put one foot on the back passenger door and pulled again at the handle of the driver's door. It finally gave and she landed in a heap in a bunch of wet leaves.

A groan came from the car and it made her heart leap. Noise was good. Noise meant that people were alive. She scrambled to her feet and leaned inside the car. Jack was checking the pulse of the woman in the passenger seat. Amber did the same with the man on her side, wrinkling her nose a little. The smell inside the car was a little unpleasant. How long had they been trapped?

Something clicked into place in her head. Top-to-toe survey. The way any doctor was supposed to assess an unknown patient. She started speaking. "Hi there. I'm Amber. I'm a doctor. I'm just going to take a look at you."

The man under her hands gave another groan

and his eyelids flickered open. She smiled at him. "Are you Aaron's parents?"

She could see the instant panic on his face. "How is he?" The words were weak and hoarse.

"He's holding steady," she replied. "I'm just glad we've found the right people." Her hands checked his arms, shoulders and chest. There was no apparent head injury, but his lower legs were pinned in place by the crumpled dashboard.

Jack had his head down low, speaking to the woman. He gently touched her arm and gave her a little shake. "Hi there. Can you hear me? I'm Jack, a doctor. How are you doing?"

His eyes met Amber's and he mouthed the words. "Color is poor."

He bent to the crumpled foot well and pulled out a purse, rifling through it until he found what he was looking for. "Bess. Bess, it's Jack. Can you open your eyes for me?" He'd pulled out a stethoscope and blood-pressure monitor from his bag and Amber did the same. She didn't want to move Aaron's dad's position in the seat, so she just had to wrap the cuff around his covered arm to try and get some kind of reading. She fol-lowed Jack's example and put her hand inside his jacket pocket, pulling out his wallet and checking for his forename. "Maleko… Maleko, can you open your eyes for me again?"

The man grunted and opened his eyes. "Can you tell me where you're hurting? Any pain around your neck or shoulders?"

He shook his head slightly, then groaned loudly and pointed to his legs. She glanced up at Jack. "It's difficult to see because of the collapsed foot well." She pulled on a pair of gloves and gently felt with her hands. When she brought her hand back out it was covered in blood.

"I think we might need some help getting him out of here. Looks like a fractured tib and fib. I'll give him something for the pain. What about you?"

Jack's brow was creased. "I could really do with some oxygen. I'm thinking she's got some kind of chest injury, either from the seat belt or from the airbag. Probably a punctured lung." His gaze met hers. "Can you give me a minute until I radio in and try and get some support from Fire and Rescue? We're going to need help getting them out of the car."

Amber nodded and edged further into the car

so she could keep an eye on both of the patients. Maybe opening the doors hadn't been such a good idea. The heavy rain was driving hard against her back. She reached over and touched Bess's face. "Hold on, Bess. Aaron's waiting for you. I know he'll be so happy to hear both of your voices."

Her stomach twisted and coiled. She couldn't go through this again. She couldn't be the person who had to tell a family that their relatives had been lost in a desperate attempt to reach their child on time—particularly when she still didn't know what the outcome for Aaron would be. It was all just too much.

The hurricane. The fear. The worry about whether she was good enough. The injuries well outside her area of expertise. And Jack. The first man she'd kissed in forever. A doctor. He should have a red flashing warning light above his head to tell her to stay away. But she'd kissed him anyway. What was she thinking?

She reached into her bag to find some pain relief for Maleko, and to try and squeeze some wound pads in next to him to stem the slow flow of blood. If she knew he didn't have a spinal injury, she could help remove his jacket and get a true blood-pressure reading. But she didn't have that guarantee right now. She didn't have a cervical collar or a spinal board, let alone any cutting equipment to release his legs from the cramped space they were trapped in.

Jack was still busy on the radio. He hadn't climbed back into the vehicle and she could see the rain drenching him as he stood in front of the headlights. She sucked in a breath. From his gestures, she could tell he was annoyed. He didn't like not being in charge. He didn't like not having complete control. She could sense all these things even from here. The resolute single-mindedness and obsession with the job were written all over his face.

It was so reminiscent of her father that it almost felt like a punch to the stomach.

She closed her eyes for the briefest of seconds. She was soaked now too. The rain was running down her face and cheeks, hiding the tears that were sneaking out alongside. She'd kissed this man. For a brief second she'd felt connected to this man—even though every part of her being told her to run in the other direction.

He'd told her about his girlfriend. He'd had his heart broken. Chewed up and destroyed by a set of circumstances that he'd had no control over. That on any other day might never have happened.

How did a guy who at heart was a control freak get over that?

How many nights had he spent awake asking the what-if questions?

She ducked her head back inside the car and rechecked Maleko's obs. "We're trying to get some more help. Hopefully you'll be a bit more comfortable until we can get you out of here."

She frowned as she looked at Bess's complexion once more. Were her lips slightly more blue? She pulled out her flashlight. The headlights from the other car just weren't strong enough and she needed to see a little better.

Darn it. Bess looked terrible. She clambered through the muddy ground around the car, her rubber boots almost being pulled from her feet. Jack was still arguing with someone on the radio.

She pulled out her stethoscope and slid it under Bess's jumper. Definite decreased breath sounds on the right-hand side. It was likely that she'd broken one or more ribs. There was a good chance one had pierced her lung and caused it to collapse. Trouble was, she had no idea of Bess's medical history. She knelt down and watched for a few seconds. All of Bess's accessory muscles were trying to pull air into her body. While a collapsed lung would always cause problems, most people would still be able to get enough air through their other lung. Could Bess be asthmatic? Where had Jack put that purse?

She rummaged around the floor again and emptied the contents of the bag out onto the ground next to her, shining down with her flashlight to get a better view.

"What on earth are you doing?" came the angry voice.

"Quiet, Jack." A wallet, lipstick, credit cards, pens, a phone with a cracked screen and about ten missed calls, a strip of paracetamol, another blister pack of blood-pressure meds and, yes, an inhaler.

She picked it up and checked it, then gave it a shake. Jack sounded annoyed now. "Can you let me back in?"

It was clear he wasn't really paying attention

to what she was doing—partly because the car door was blocking his view. She flipped the cap off the inhaler. "Bess, I'm going to give you a few puffs of your inhaler. I know you can't really breathe in properly, so just try and get as much as you can."

Bess was aware enough to form her lips around the inhaler as Amber administered the medication.

Jack obviously lost patience and nudged her with his shoulder as he tried to see what she was doing. But Amber wasn't having any of it.

She rooted her feet to the sticky ground and held firm. "That's right, Bess. You're doing great. Let's see if your breathing eases a little while we wait for some help."

She shot Jack a dirty look as she straightened up and pulled her head out of the car. "Back off, Jack. I'm just as capable a doctor as you. You can't be in charge of everything."

Even as she said the words, she felt an instant pang of regret. The flash of pain across his face—her recognition of what he'd revealed earlier. She understood the theory of why he had an inbuilt feeling of wanting to be in control. She just couldn't live with it.

They were incompatible in every which way.

Even though she wanted to reach up and brush some of the rain from his face right now. Even though as she looked at his lips all she could remember was that kiss.

She'd gathered confidence in the last few hours that she wouldn't let anyone take away from her—not even Jack Campbell.

An hour later Ron looked at them both as they climbed out of the back of the fire truck. The ER was swarming with people. Some clearly patients, others with a whole variety of colored tabards on. It almost made her head ache as much as her body currently did.

"Oh, my missing docs." Ron looked over as the patients were unloaded. He seemed much more comfortable now he could focus only on his ER. "What have we got?"

Amber spoke first. "This is Bess and Maleko. They were on their way from Hilo and were involved in a car accident." Ron opened his mouth to interject but Amber kept talking. "Their son Aaron is one of the teenagers with meningitis."

"Ah…" Ron's eyebrows rose.

"Maleko has fractured his left tib and fib and had to be cut out of the car. He's had ten of morphine at the scene around an hour ago. Bess is asthmatic and looks like she has a right-sided pneumothorax. Her color has only improved since she had some Ventolin, but she's been struggling with her breathing since we found them."

She was conscious of Jack standing behind her. She could almost feel him itching to talk but she was determined to do the handover properly.

Ron didn't seem to notice any issue. He just turned and issued instructions. "Him, Cubicle Three, and her, Resus Room Four. Get me a portable chest X-ray and a chest tube tray. Find me a surgeon for Cubicle Three."

He turned to face them again. "Quick question. They're expecting to have some emergency flights available tomorrow for any tourists that want to leave. I can't tell you what to do. But the next week or so will be mad. We'll move into disaster relief and emergency services mode. I still need doctors. Any kind of doctors. All kinds of doctors. And don't expect to be paid. So, do have someplace you need to be in the next few days, or can you stay?"

"I'll stay."

"I'll stay."

There was no hesitation. Their voices sounded in perfect unison. And Amber turned on her heel and locked gazes with Jack.

Both of them looked in surprise at the other.

Her heart gave a couple of flips. What had possessed her? But as she looked around the crowded ER, she knew exactly why she'd agreed.

This wasn't about her. This wasn't about Jack.

But that still didn't explain the fact she was secretly glad he'd also said yes.

CHAPTER SEVEN

BY THE TIME they reached the apartment that had been designated to emergency rescue workers, both of them were ready to collapse with exhaustion. Another emergency worker glanced at them as he was about to leave. He threw them a set of keys. "Your room is the one at the back. I hope you brought some extra scrubs. We've no spare clothes."

He disappeared out of the door and they were left staring at each other. Jack shrugged. "Your room" made it sound like one room. Amber walked down the dark corridor and pushed open the door. Sure enough, there was one—not particularly big—double bed.

"I'll sleep on the floor," said Jack quickly. He didn't want to make her uncomfortable—even though they'd kissed. It was clear Amber still had issues with him.

Amber shook her head. The moon was the

only light in the room at present. "Don't be silly, Jack. I'm tired. You're tired."

She gave a half shrug. "After all, we've managed to share a bed before." She held out her hands. "We could be here for the next few days. Let's not make things difficult."

He glanced around. "It's a pretty small space." He knew exactly what she was saying. They hadn't had an official fight, but things just seemed uneasy between them.

She nodded. "It is. So let's make the best of it."

He gave a resigned nod as he stripped off his jacket. "Fine by me."

He tried to keep his face neutral. Last time he'd shared a bed with Amber, he'd barely known her, but had been acting on the flirting and glimmer of attraction between them. She hadn't known his hang-ups and he hadn't known hers. This was different. This was another step. They'd already kissed. In among this disaster there was something in the air between them. Something he hadn't quite managed to get his head around yet. He knew he acted like a control freak sometimes. He knew that Amber had her No Doctor rule in her head. But where did that really leave them?

"Fine by me." Amber's words echoed his as she sat down at the edge of the bed and took off her boots.

Jack smiled at the back of her head. They'd reached an uneasy truce, and somehow he knew he wouldn't sleep a wink.

She was sharing a room with Jack Campbell. In the midst of chaos someone had obviously decided they were together and given them a temporary room in an apartment—the hotel was literally under siege as it now had to accommodate people who had lost their homes. So it had seemed churlish to object.

Lack of power was still the main issue. The power companies were working hard to safely restore power to the island. But they were stretched beyond capacity. And safety was more important than being able to turn on your lights at night.

But it meant that nights could be long.

They'd reached an easy compromise. They worked wherever the disaster relief coordinator sent them. Her little outburst and subsequent bristliness couldn't be helped. The work was constant and exhausting. She'd managed to track down all of the close contacts for meningitis and ensure they had antibiotics. Aaron now seemed to be on the slow road to recovery. Zane's progress was picking up. For a short while there had been a question over septicemia and how it was affecting his hands and feet. But the blood flow had improved and the toxins seemed to be leaving his system.

Amber was still concerned that in among the chaos there could be more cases that might be overlooked. There were so many voluntary agencies now that coordination of information seemed nigh on impossible.

Her director at the DPA had supported her decision to stay for the next week and told her that he trusted her. That meant a lot.

"Amber, do you know if we have any food in this place?"

It had been four days since the hurricane. By the time they got back to the apartment at night they were too tired to even talk. Most of the local businesses were waiting for insurance assessments before opening again, and there was only one tiny corner shop that had managed to open its doors.

Jack was staring at a box of cornflakes they'd eaten for the last two days straight. It was empty.

"I think we had soup." She walked across the kitchen and opened a cupboard. Empty. There were four other emergency service workers sharing the apartment—any one of them could have eaten it. "Maybe not." She shrugged as she closed the door. Her stomach grumbled loudly.

She put her hands on the counter and stretched out her sore back. "I guess the only place we can go is back to the hospital, or to one of the evacuation centers. At least we know the school kitchens are open."

Jack pulled a face. "Is it wrong if I say I can't stand the noise?" He rubbed his eyes. "I've spent most of the day surrounded by bedlam. I'd kind of like five minutes of quiet."

She paused for a second as Jack's stomach grumbled loudly then burst out laughing. "Well, there's no food at the inn. So, we have to go somewhere. Hospital or school?"

He sighed. "Okay, then." He grabbed the keys

for the emergency vehicle they were still using. "Let's go to the school."

Ten minutes later they reached the high school that was still doubling as an evacuation center. Although all people who were evacuated when there was a hurricane had been told to bring enough food with them for seven days, the logistics of trying to store and manage that amount of food was more difficult than anyone had previously predicted.

After two days, the high-school kitchens had been opened with volunteers and aid agencies cooking in shifts. Further emergency supplies of food and bottled water had been shipped in so that no one was left hungry or thirsty.

Jack was right. It was beyond noisy. A constant clamor of people all trying to be heard above one another. Amber noticed a little family holed up in a corner, a dark-eyed woman trying to get two small children to sleep on a mat and blankets on the floor. "What must it be like in here at night? Do you think all these people have damaged houses?"

Jack seemed to follow her gaze. "Maybe. One area had some flash flooding too. I was down helping earlier today. Some of the houses were virtually washed away."

She frowned. She'd spent part of the day in ER, part with Aaron and Zane, and part in a temporary clinic. It was hard to keep track of everything. "What were you doing there?"

"It's a bit further away and some of the people were desperately trying to salvage what they could from their homes. Lots of dirty water, some of it waist-high."

Amber nodded. "Dirty water, dirty wounds. High chance of infections."

"Exactly."

They joined the line for food at the kitchen. Jack picked up a couple of bottles of water for them both. "How much longer will you stay?"

She shook her head. "I don't know. The director was happy for me to stay for a week in the first instance. But I don't know how much leeway I'll get after that. What about you?"

"I'm officially on leave. Holidays. Then I need to look for another job. So I can stay as long as I'm needed."

She pressed her lips together and nodded. "I

heard Ron asking you earlier about surgeries. Are you going to help out?"

He nodded. "Probably starting tomorrow. There are lots of bone injuries and I got loads of orthopedic experience in Afghanistan. One of the hospital surgeons was injured himself, and another's had an MI. So, they're kind of desperate."

They reached the front of the line and took the plates offered to them. Amber lifted the plate to her nose and inhaled. "It's some kind of curry. It smells great."

All the seats were taken, so they walked back through the foyer and outside. For the first time in days the rain had finally stopped. The sky was dark again but now they could see a smattering of stars glistening above.

Amber looked from side to side. Disaster still echoed around them. Remnants of the roof were still lying on the football field. A few broken windows in the school were boarded up. But the wind that had whipped around them for days had eventually died down and the night seemed almost peaceful, even if the place around them wasn't.

They walked over and sat on one of the stone walls near the front of the school. The car park behind them was littered with emergency vehicles and cars.

They ate in silence for a few minutes. "When do you think this will ever get back to normal? I can't believe that the beautiful place we landed in a few days ago has changed so much."

Jack stopped eating and put down his plastic fork. "I didn't even really get a chance to appreciate the beauty due to the jet lag. My eyes were closed the whole way from the airport. Seems like such a waste now."

Amber sighed. "I heard in the hospital today that a hotel on one of the other islands collapsed. We're lucky that didn't happen here." She held up one hand. "But look now. The rain and wind have gone. If we were lying on the grass right now looking up at the sky, we might think that nothing had ever happened."

There was a loud clatter and some raised voices behind them. Jack smiled and glanced over his shoulder. "Yeah, and then you hear the noise."

Amber nodded in agreement. "Yeah, the noise. Or how different it is."

"What do you mean?"

She smiled. "I mean, no mobile phones. Limited electricity. No TV. No Internet. No music."

Jack groaned. "And no real water."

Four days on there were still no mobile masts and it didn't look as if they could be replaced anytime soon. None of the regular utilities were working properly and the apartment they were staying in only had water switched on for two hours a day. It meant limited showering and limited toilet facilities.

"I can't wait to get back to a hotel at some point and just stand in the shower for an hour."

Jack laughed. "I don't see that happening in the next few days. I'm not sure we'll even get back to the hotel. Did you leave anything important there?"

Amber couldn't help but pull a face. "Just business suits, other clothes and my laptop. Nothing that can't be replaced. There's only one thing I'm keen to get back and it's a locket my mom gave me for my twenty-first birthday. I'd left it in the safe." She turned to face him on the wall. "What about you?"

He blinked for a second and breathed out slowly. "Like you, clothes, a laptop."

"And?" She knew. She just knew there was something else.

He stared up into the sky for a few moments. "It's nothing that I couldn't replace. It's just…"

"Just what?"

He looked back down and stared at the plate still in his hands. "A photo. A photo of Jill from years ago. She's sitting in the camp in her army fatigues, laughing at something someone said. We had quite a lot of photos together. You know, it's a modern world. Everyone has a phone constantly. But after…the photo that made me catch my breath was this one. We're not in it together. I have no idea what we were doing at the time. Probably just taking a five-minute break between scrubbing for Theater. But it's her. It captured her essence, the person who she was."

Amber bit her lip. Her heart ached for him. The grief seemed raw. Was that wrong two years on?

But before she had a chance to say anything, Jack continued. "I know it's stupid. It's just a photo. I don't carry it in my wallet. It's in my suitcase." He let out a wry laugh. "Jill would call me an idiot. But, sometimes, when I get carried away with things, it helps to remind me why I do this."

"You do this for her?"

He leaned forward and put his plate on the ground, then rested his head in his hands. "I do this for them all." He turned his head toward her and looked sideways through wounded eyes. "The wound dressing—the science behind it. It was all so much easier than realizing I'd lost Jill." His voice broke and he sat up and held out his hands. "I don't even know what would have happened. We might have stayed together. We may have grown apart. The one thing I am sure of is that we would always have been friends."

Her heart twisted inside her chest. She'd never felt a pull to someone like that she felt toward Jack Campbell. It didn't matter that it was all wrong. It didn't matter what her brain told her. What made her heart twist was the fact she was sitting with him and he was talking about another woman. One who'd obviously meant a lot to him.

"Friends is good," she said, trying to keep any emotion from her voice.

Jack kept his brown gaze fixed on her. "Is it?"

Her skin prickled. "What do you mean?"

"Are we friends?"

She shifted on the wall. "Well, I'm not sure…" Her brain couldn't think straight. Was that the word she would use for the guy she'd met barely a few days before, shared a bed with, kissed and quarreled with? "Are we?"

Jack was leaning forward, his elbows resting on his knees, his gaze unwavering from hers. When he spoke his voice was hoarse. "What if, for the first time in a long time, I've looked at someone and wanted to be more than friends?"

The words swept over her skin. Half warming, half making every tiny hair on her body stand on end. Was that even possible?

Her hands automatically crossed her body and started running up and down her arms. "But I don't date doctors." It was like her default answer. She'd been saying it for so long that her brain found it easiest to resort to the familiar.

"I know. But you kiss them."

Her mouth opened. She hadn't quite expected him to be so direct. "You kissed me."

"You kissed me back." He straightened. There was a glint in his eye that seemed to be highlighted by the stars above them.

The world around them was a wreck. They were both wrecks.

But underneath them and underneath the land around them was a beauty that was hinting to get back out—to get back to the surface and let itself be revealed.

He drew in a deep breath. She tried so hard not to let her eyes fall to his broad shoulders and chest. To drink in the stubble on his jaw, and the way the expression in his eyes was so deep it just seemed to pull her in, like some kind of leash.

"I don't know what this is." The edges of his lips curled upward. "I know that our timing sucks. I know you think you shouldn't date a work-obsessed doctor." He put his hand on his chest. "I know that I've spent the last two years virtually avoiding all contact with anyone of the opposite sex. Some might call me work-obsessed." He ran one hand through his hair.

"But it's so much easier to focus on work. To let it take over. To let it consume all your thoughts."

She frowned. "I'm not sure you're doing a good job of convincing me that we should be friends."

He nodded and stood up, stepping in front of her and gently taking her by the elbows so she was facing him. They were only a few inches apart.

"How about if I tell you that I'm confused? How about if I tell you that my judgment may be skewed by hurricanes, lack of sleep, lack of food, forced proximity and a hypnotic smell of rose and orange that seems to follow me around?"

Her scent. He was talking about her perfume. She couldn't help but smile. "I'm still not sure about the friends thing. I have standards, you know."

"What kind of standards?"

"You know, they have to like the same books, the same movies and, most importantly, the same chocolate."

"Ah." He raised his eyebrows. "These could be impossibly high standards. I could be suspicious that you're trying to stack the odds against me because I'm a doctor."

She smiled and shook her head. "Quit stalling for time."

He lifted his hands and rested them gently on the tops of her arms. "The answers would have to be crime, sci-fi and...a kind of chocolate that is only available in Scotland. I'm very loyal."

She wrinkled her brow and gave her head a shake. "Oh, no, we're not a good match for friends at all. It has to be romance, action movies and old-fashioned American chocolate bars every single time."

He smiled and leaned a little closer. "I have another way we can check our compatibility level."

"You do?" Now she could smell him. A mixture of earthy tones and soap.

His eyes were serious but he was still smiling. And she couldn't help but smile too. She slid her hands up his chest as he leaned in toward her, and she tilted her chin up toward him. This time there was no dark store closet.

This time there was a background of noise, and a smattering of stars in the sky. Last time around things had been more tentative. This time, Jack didn't hesitate. His lips were on hers straightaway. His fingers tangling through her loose hair, tugging her even closer to him.

She breathed in, pushing all the confusing thoughts from her head. She knew exactly where she was. She knew exactly what she was doing.

It didn't make a bit of sense to her. But she'd spent the last few days with this man at her side. And even though they weren't together, even though they weren't a couple and even though he carried a photo of someone else in his suitcase, she still didn't want to step from his arms.

His kisses were sure, pulling her in and making her want more. His body was pressed against hers; all she could feel were the strong muscular planes next to her curves. It wasn't often that she met a man who wasn't intimidated by her height. In general she could look most men square in the eyes. On a few occasions, heels had been a complete no-no on a date. But with Jack she had to tip her head upward to meet his lips. Her eyes barely came to his shoulders.

As he kissed her, his hands slid from her hair to her waist. If she were anywhere else she might be tempted to wrap her legs around him, but somehow, in the middle of a disaster, and in front of a school, it just didn't seem appropriate.

She actually laughed and took a step back.

"What? What is it?" Jack glanced around as if he'd missed something.

She shook her head and held out her hands. "We're in front of a school that's currently an evacuation center for around two thousand people. And… I'm still trying to decide if we are friends or not." She was smiling as she said the words. Parts of her brain were screaming, but other parts of her were warm.

Jack sounded ready to move on. It seemed as though he'd looked inside and realized he'd spent too long blocking out the world and just focusing on work. Maybe now he would take a breather and decide what he wanted to do next.

That could be anywhere, with anyone. But that flicker of something she'd felt that first night in the bar was igniting wildly.

So when he held out his hand toward her she didn't hesitate to take it.

CHAPTER EIGHT

HE'D KISSED HER. He'd kissed her again and again even though his brain couldn't seem to formulate any clear thoughts.

Then they'd gone back to the apartment and kissed some more.

They'd fallen asleep with their arms wrapped around each other just as they had the first night. Except Jack hadn't slept much.

He'd been too busy caught between staring at the woman in the bed next to him and looking out of the window at the bright stars above.

He felt…different. He'd spent so long focused on work and shielding his heart from any hurt that he'd never even thought about connecting with someone again.

And this had just crept up on him. Out of nowhere, really. One minute he was jet-lagged at a bar; next he was focused on the woman with the pink-tipped hair striding across the ballroom.

And everything after that he just couldn't really work out.

This was a woman who had told him straight-out she wasn't interested. She didn't date doctors, ever. But the sparks that had flown at the first meeting had never died. No matter what she said.

She was a good doctor. Conscientious. Caring. Even when completely out of her depth. No wonder she was doing so well at the DPA. They were lucky to have her.

His stomach gave a few flip-flops as he thought about what came next. He hadn't been able to access emails for days. He'd been having a few tentative exchanges about job possibilities. He'd need to make a decision soon.

Amber groaned and shifted position, her arm draping across his chest. He wanted to nudge and kiss her awake. Every cell in his body was currently screaming at him. But he couldn't do that. Not like this.

They'd been pushed into a forced proximity. It didn't matter how much of a pull he felt toward Amber. After waiting two years to connect with someone, he wanted to be sure. And he wanted *her* to be sure. Because Amber Berkeley gave off a whole host of conflicting signals. Oh, sure, she kissed really well. But just because she kissed him didn't mean she wanted anything to progress between them. And how did you have that conversation with someone you'd really only just met?

Amber moved again, her lips brushing against the skin at his shoulder. Jack almost groaned out loud.

One thing was clear. Carrying on like this would drive him plain crazy.

Amber checked the obs chart in front of her. Aaron was on his way to a good recovery. Zane was finally making progress too, allowing her to breathe a big sigh of relief.

Jack came up behind her. "How you doing?"

He'd been a little awkward this morning. Not unpleasant. Just a little brisker than before. When she'd woken up and found herself wrapped around him again, all she'd been able to think of was how right things felt.

By the time she'd got her five-minute shower she'd tried to be more sensible. In a few days she'd have to leave and get back to Chicago and the DPA. Jack still had no idea what to do next. And she'd no right to have an opinion on anything about that.

He nudged her again. "Hey? Are you with me?" His voice was soft, like velvet touching her skin, and she jerked back to attention.

"What? Yes. I've just finished checking on Aaron's mom. Her lung has reinflated and she's feeling a lot better."

Jack nodded. "I checked his dad. The pins in his tib and fib look good. He's got a walking cast on and they've had him on his feet already. Once he's mastered the hospital stairs on his crutches, he'll be good to go."

"Aaron should be ready to go in a few days. I've taken some more bloods this morning and he seems to be responding to the antibiotics well."

Jack gave a nod. "How about if I told you that I managed to find a shop that's opened?"

"Really?" That had her instant attention. She wanted to buy some toiletries and some food. Probably in that order.

He nodded again. "Apparently they had a delivery today from the mainland. They have some fresh food. I might have bought some."

"You might have bought some?" She arched an eyebrow at him. "What exactly *might* you have bought?"

"Chicken. Potatoes. Veg. Bread. Butter."

She rolled her eyes upward. "Sounds like heaven. Do we get to eat this food in a place that doesn't hold two thousand other people?" She wrinkled her nose. "And smell like two thousand other people."

"Oh, yeah," breathed Jack. "I also heard a rumor that the utilities might be turned on for a bit longer tonight. We might get more than an hour of water."

"Now, that would really be bliss." She leaned back against the nearest wall. Then something came into her head. "Hey, tonight, who's cooking? Shall we flip for it?"

He gave a sneaky kind of smile. "Well, since I managed to find the food…"

She shook her head. "Oh, no. Oh, no, you don't. We flip for it."

"Or?"

"Or I steal the food and eat it myself."

He pulled a quarter from his pocket. "Okay, then. Heads or tails?"

"Tails."

He flipped the coin. It spun in the air and landed on his palm.

She grinned. "Tails." She lifted one finger and prodded his shoulder. "Just remember. I prefer barbecue chicken. Or maybe chicken cordon bleu."

She gave her stomach a little rub to tease him.

He shook his head. "Don't let it be said that anyone calls you Bossy Britches."

She batted her eyelashes. "Dr. Campbell, I have absolutely no idea what you mean."

He was strangely nervous. And he had no idea why. He was a perfectly capable cook. He could throw together a dinner without too many problems—even with his eyes on the clock to make sure he coordinated it with the bursts of power. The apartment they were temporarily residing in was only a few streets away from the beach. Since there were still a number of other emergency helpers using the apartment, Jack decided it might be easier to pack up the food and take it outside.

Their belongings had been dropped off from the hotel around an hour ago. In the chaos after the hurricane, the hotel was being used as a temporary shelter for some families. It seemed that his belongings had been more or less thrown into the case. But everything seemed to be there.

He undid the zipper on the inside lid of the case and slipped his hand inside. The wave of relief passed over his body instantly as he felt the battered edge of the photograph, but he froze as he went to pull it out. He knew it was there. He knew he hadn't lost it. But he'd lost her.

Did he need to keep looking at her photograph?

His fingers released the edge of the photograph as he knelt by the case. He breathed for a minute. In. Out. In. Out.

He pulled back his hand and fixed his eyes on the door. He'd used to have the picture on permanent display. That had stopped a few months ago. Would he ever get rid of it? No. Never.

He would always be respectful of Jill's memories. Her life. Her love. Her laughter.

But in the last few days it was as if the shadows had lifted from his eyes. And from his heart.

His head had stopped focusing only on the research. He'd never been interested in the business side of things. He'd only ever been interested in developing the best product that might actually save lives. Now he'd done it and he had the evidence base to prove it. But his obsession had started to diminish.

Today, he'd finally managed to access a working computer for a few minutes. Seven hundred emails. Mostly about the wound dressing.

But the only ones that he'd opened had been the emails about job opportunities. Doctors Without Borders. Seven private clinics throughout the world. Six NHS posts highlighted to him by friends and colleagues who thought he would be suitable. Three possible aid agencies postings in far-off places that would be similar to what he was actually doing right now in Hawaii.

He'd always thought he'd know the right job opportunity as soon as it came along. But somehow, in among all of this, for the first time he was uncertain.

He'd always had a career path in his head. Up

until this point it had served him well. But now? Here, in Hawaii, with his senses awakening for the first time in years, he just didn't know what path to take.

The door banged and Amber walked in. She was wearing a pair of thin blue scrubs with her hair tied up on top of her head. Her eyes widened as she saw him crouched on the floor. "Our luggage? We have our luggage?"

He nodded, and before he got a chance to point her bright green suitcase out, she'd spotted it and ran across the floor, throwing herself on top of it. "Come to Mama, clean clothes, shampoo and moisturizer." She laughed as he shook his head at her while she stayed in position.

"What? Are you trying to tell me that you haven't craved your own clean shirt and underwear in the last few days?"

She jumped up and dragged her case toward the bathroom. "Leave me alone. I might be some time." Her eyes were gleaming.

He smiled and stood up, waiting for a few seconds until he heard the inevitable signs of the shower running. He lifted his hand and knocked on the door.

"What?" came the impatient shout.

He leaned on the wall and folded his arms across his chest as he kept grinning. "Amber? Just to let you know, you have—" he glanced at his watch "—nine minutes."

"What?" Her horror-struck face appeared at a tiny gap in the door. "Tell me you're joking?"

He tapped his watch as he walked away. "Tick, tick, Amber."

It was the quickest shower in the history of the world. She'd been vaguely aware of the smell of cooking food as she'd entered the apartment, but the sight of her suitcase had been too good. When she'd flung it open inside the bathroom there had been a note on the top asking her to collect her valuables from the hotel and to bring her passport with her. That had to mean that they'd emptied the safe in her room and taken her locket someplace else.

She ran across the hallway with only a towel wrapped around her so she could blast her hair with the hair dryer. Sure enough, in around two minutes, the lights and power flickered off. She let out a groan. Jack appeared at the door smiling, dressed in a T-shirt and jeans. "What? You didn't quite make it in time?"

She threw back her still-damp hair. "Darn it. At least I've got rid of some of the wetness." She frowned as she remembered the state of the clothes in the bathroom. "But I think I'm going to look like some kind of dishrag tonight. I wasn't able to iron any of my clothes."

Jack gave her a steady glance. "I think you'll look fine, no matter what you're wearing."

A little tingle ran over her skin. There were a few flickering candles in the main room but very little other light. She licked her lips and wondered if she could put on some makeup in the virtual darkness. It was almost as if he read her mind. He strode through the main room and walked back with a candle. "Here. You'll need it to get dressed. I'll pack up the food in the kitchen."

She was surprised. "Aren't we eating here?"

He gave her a wicked glance. "We're sharing with four other people—what's the chances of them coming in and stealing our food? The beach nearby looks safe enough. I thought we could eat down there and pretend we were still in the Hawaii we came to."

She reached out and took the flickering candle as her stomach gave a little squeeze. "Give me five minutes. That's all I'll take."

And she did. Grabbing a red beach dress from her case that she'd planned to wear for a more casual day, and a pair of flat sandals. Her hair was still damp but she left it around her shoulders in the hope it might dry in the warm evening air. Finally she slicked on some red lipstick as she squinted in the mirror in the candlelight then grabbed a light black cardigan.

When she walked back out in the corridor, Jack was standing with a package wrapped in aluminum foil in one hand and a bottle in the other. She laughed and shook her head as she walked up. "What? No wicker basket? No picnic rug or crystal glasses?"

"I'm all out." He shrugged. "This is going to be more like some high-school midnight feast than some big seduction scene."

She stepped forward, closer than she would normally dare. They were currently alone. The only light was the flickering candles. "Is that what this is?" she asked teasingly. "A big seduction scene?"

Jack's pupils seemed to dilate a little. She liked that. She liked that a lot.

He gave the slightest raise of his eyebrows and dared to lean a little closer, letting her inhale the dark woody aftershave he'd put on.

He adjusted his package and held one hand palm up. "Let's see. We've already shared a bed—how many times? We've kissed." He gave a little smile. "Maybe twice. Do we need a seduction scene?"

She was fixed on his eyes. Had he always had such thick eyelashes? Why was she just noticing them now? She licked her lips subconsciously. "You can't seduce me," she said, her voice more hoarse than she'd expected. "I don't date doctors, remember?"

He slid his arm around her waist and pulled her closer. "Who said anything about dating?"

Maybe it was the dim lighting. Maybe it was the slow buildup of momentum in their mutual attraction. Maybe it was the combination of reasons that they shouldn't really be together.

But whatever their pasts, whatever the world had against them, it seemed that somewhere above those stars had aligned for tonight.

They walked down to the beach with her hand tucked inside his elbow. The tidy-up around them had started. There were lots of areas still needing attention. Buildings still requiring massive repairs. The path to the beach had a number of heavily bent palm trees, one appeared to have been completely torn from its roots, but other than that there were no major issues. The beach was deserted, just a pale expanse of sand and a virtually black sea.

Jack had grabbed a towel from the apartment so they had something to sit on. They settled down and he eased the aluminum foil open. The crinkling sound seemed to echo around them.

Amber bent down and inhaled, her hair falling around her and shielding her face. He resisted the temptation to reach out and pull it back. She sat back up, smiling. "You made it. Barbecue chicken." Her eyes were gleaming in the pale moonlight. "You actually made it."

"Of course I did. You requested it." He gave a simple shrug as he handed her one of the plates that he'd brought from the kitchen. It only took a few moments to share out the chicken and potato salad that he'd made. Ingredients had been few but it was still better than eating at the evacuation center. He also opened the wine he'd acquired at the nearby shop.

"Darn it." He shook his head. "We have no glasses."

Amber gave him a fake look of horror. "You mean we'll have to drink from the bottle? How classy." She shook her head as she took the bottle from his hands and expertly removed the cork with the bottle opener. "Do you honestly think I'm that kind of girl?" She winked and put the bottle to her lips, extending her neck and tipping her head back, giving him a perfect view of her profile in the moonlight.

He caught his breath. It had been a long time since that had happened—in fact, had it ever happened before? In the space of a few days Amber Berkeley had started to burrow her way under his skin. He'd found himself looking for her constantly. Picking up on the sound of her voice, even when they weren't in the same room. Wondering what she thought of him. And that last kiss—it had haunted him. In more ways than one…

Amber handed the bottle back to him, still smiling, then leaned back on her hands and sighed. "Wow."

"Wow?"

She nodded. "Yeah. Look around. From here we can hardly see any sign of the damage. Just a beautiful beach with a mile of sand, an endless dark ocean with stars in the sky above." She nodded in appreciation. "This is the Hawaii I imagined coming to. The one I had in my head. The daytime being yellow sand, bright blue ocean and a multitude of colored flowers, and the nighttime being beautiful, quiet and romantic."

Jack smiled as he shifted to face her. "Romantic?"

From here she was bathed in the pale moonlight. It caressed her skin, showing the glow and the vitality. She closed her eyes for a second and breathed again. Then turned her head to face him. "Yes. Romantic."

He paused. "What happens next, Amber?"

She licked her lips. He knew exactly what he wanted her to say.

She shifted on her hips so they were face on. She hadn't stopped smiling. "I guess I'm not entirely sure. The last few days have been... strange."

"Strange?"

She held up her hands. "Challenging. In a whole host of ways. Challenging for work. Challenging for life and...challenging for me."

He could tell she needed to talk out loud. He nodded. "It's been...different. I didn't come here expecting to find anything."

"And have you?" Her eyes were wide with expectation.

He put his hand up to his chest. "I feel like I have. I came here wondering what came next. I came here just to present at the conference—to tell the rest of the world about our product. And that was it. That was all that I was here to do."

"So what happened?" There was a teasing edge in her tone.

He met her twinkling gaze. "I met an unstoppable force. And it made me feel as if I found a little bit of myself again."

"You did?" Her voice broke.

He nodded slowly as he licked his lips. "*She* made me feel as if I found a little bit of myself again."

Amber moved. She hitched up her dress and put one leg over him, so she was sitting facing him.

"This is getting to be a habit," said Jack hoarsely.

She slid her arms around his neck and tipped her head to the side. "I think it might be."

His hands went to her waist. "Maybe we need to rethink your rule. Don't most people say that rules were made to be broken?"

She lowered her head and whispered in his ear. "How about you convince me?"

"I think I can do that…"

And he did.

CHAPTER NINE

THE DOOR TO the room burst open. Amber sat bolt upright in the bed then remembered she didn't have quite as many clothes on as she usually did. Kino, one of the emergency workers who was sharing their apartment, only momentarily blinked. "Amber, Jack. You're needed. We've all been called in."

Jack moved seamlessly. He stood up, grabbed a set of scrubs that were lying on the floor and stepped into them. He pulled on his shoes and immediately started asking questions. "What is it? What's happened?"

Amber was still in the process of waking up and Jack was already dressed. Of course. An army doc. He was used to emergency calls. She'd never been good at the intern hours of putting your head on the pillow only for a page to sound yet again.

Kino kept talking. "A landslide. It's caught one

of the villages on the outskirts of Kailua Kona. Multiple casualties."

Kino moved away. "I'll wait for you outside."

As soon as he left, Amber retrieved her underwear and grabbed a clean T-shirt, jeans and sneakers. She didn't have time to worry about appearances, so she clipped her hair up on her head and met Jack at the door.

"Ready?" His face had become almost a mask. The warmth and emotion she'd glimpsed last night seemed to have been put back in their box. He seemed totally focused.

She grabbed her jacket and followed him out to the car. They were lucky they still had it on loan—and that their emergency packs were in the trunk. Jack handed her the radio as Kino climbed in their car. "Might as well come with you," he said as Jack nodded.

Jack started the engine. "Call in, Amber. See if we've to go to the hospital first, or straight onto the site."

Their instructions were clear. They were to be part of the first responders on site.

They traveled the rest of the way in virtual silence with only the occasional crackle from the radio. Kino was able to point out directions as he was from one of the other Hawaiian islands and was familiar with this area. Most of the major roads had been cleared of any fallen trees and debris by now.

But as they ventured nearer the village, the extent of the damage was evident. Four emergency vehicles were ahead of them, bright flashing lights causing Jack to slow down on the road. It was just as well, because the rest of the road had vanished in the landslide.

Amber had never seen anything like this before and she stepped out trying to survey the scene. "Where's the village?" seemed the obvious question.

Kino's voice was shaky. "It was there," he said, pointing to the mass of rubble and mud ahead of them.

Amber shook her head. "I don't get it. What's happened?"

One of the other emergency responders walked over. "It's because of the hurricane and the amount of rainfall. The earth around the volcanoes and mountains hasn't been able to stand the strain and extra pressure. It's always a risk a few days after any major event. It's just never happened before."

Her eyes were starting to pick out things in the debris. It was mainly mud and earth, along with a million uprooted trees. But in among the rest of it she could see a few things sticking out. Part of a roof of a house? A brick wall that seemed to have been carried away by the flow of the landslide.

"How many people?" she breathed.

"About five hundred," replied the first responder. He dug into his pack and pulled out tags. "Triage. That's your first duty. Red, amber and green. We'll set up the tarp emergency tents for first responders here. Find them, pull them out, assess them."

Jack had been silent this whole time—almost as if he was creating a plan in his head. A fire truck had just pulled up and the firefighters were out instantly.

Amber opened her mouth to shout over to them as the first responder put his hand up to her face. "Don't."

"What?" She was confused. She was only

going to ask if they wanted to split into groups with the doctors.

"First rule of a landslide. The first big danger is the possibility of a further landslide. Keep noise to a minimum. No shouting. Only use the radios we'll give you." He pointed up to the mountainside. "There's always a chance that not everything has found its way down yet. There could be boulders, more trees, a million rocks, all waiting to slide back down here."

She felt her skin chill. She was walking into a situation she knew nothing about. Could she really do this? She took a few deep breaths. Jack had already started reorganizing things in his pack as some of the firefighters came over to join them, carrying radios. Another car pulled up and she recognized some of the staff from ER. They divided quickly into teams.

Her first few steps were tentative. The ground was unstable in places, and they were on an incline. But Amber followed the instructions she was given and moved as quickly as she could. Within minutes they found their first patient. A woman, who was half covered in mud and looked completely stunned. Half of her clothes were missing. Amber did a quick check and nodded to the firefighters that she was safe to move. "I was in the bathroom," the woman whispered. "I was getting dressed."

"Anyone else in your home?" asked Jack quickly.

She shook her head and Jack moved rapidly on as two of the firefighters assisted the woman back up to the almost constructed triage station.

For the next hour they worked in almost silence. Finding people trapped in the mud and earth. Some were badly injured. Others were lucky—they only had cuts and bruises. A few weren't so lucky. Amber found one man who seemed to have died of a severe head injury and another who had suffocated under the mud.

Jack was methodical and fast. He didn't waste a single second. Her stomach was in a permanent knot as she watched him. He barely acknowledged her existence. He seemed too focused on the task at hand. And she knew that was entirely how he should be. But somehow it still hurt. It still reminded her of her father. And she just couldn't shake the association.

She pulled out a child covered from head to

toe in mud. But as she bent to do a quick assessment, Jack more or less elbowed her out of the way—just as he had at the car the other night. She bristled. She couldn't help it. She was perfectly capable of assessing this child. But was now really the time to fight about it?

She left him and moved on to the next spot where a firefighter was waving over to her. He pointed downward. "We've got a house buried under here." He had his ear pressed to the ground. "We think this is part of the chimney stack. Or it used to be. Is it maybe wrong way up? Who knows. We can hear them beneath us."

"Can you get them out?" She was currently up to her knees in sticky mud. The thought of being trapped underneath that made her feel queasy.

The firefighter nodded. "The space looks wide enough. I'm going to send someone down."

"Is that safe?"

His eyes scanned the surroundings. "Is anything here?"

She swallowed and stood to the side, allowing the firefighters to sort out their gear and lower their colleague. After a few minutes the guy radioed back up. "I've got four. All badly injured.

Two adults and two kids. Can you lower me a cage? I'll need to strap them in one at a time."

It was a painstaking operation. The cage was carried over from one of the specialist fire and rescue trucks. First to come up was a woman whose color was verging on gray. She took the briefest seconds to assess. "Flail chest." Amber put a red tag on her. "Straight to hospital whatever way you can get her there."

The next up was a little girl with an ugly fracture of her arm, sticking through her skin. She was wailing at the top of her voice, making everyone nearby look around anxiously. Amber calculated in her head the little girl's size and weight. She hated approximating but it was the only way to try and ensure a safe dose of analgesia. Twenty seconds later she gave the little girl an injection to try and relieve her pain and handed her over to another firefighter to take her away. The next child was unconscious but breathing steadily. There was a slight graze to his head. She tagged him as amber and sent him on.

"There's a problem down here," came the crackle of the radio.

"What is it?"

"I can't move him. He's pinned down and I can't get him free. I need some assistance and he looks in a bad way."

Amber didn't hesitate. "Send me down. Let me look after him."

The firefighter frowned. "I'm not sure. Things are too unstable."

"You let your own man go down there—and you'll probably have to send another." She was determined. She was a doctor. This was her role and she wanted to play her part.

"I don't know." The firefighter hesitated.

"Well, I do. Where's a harness? Get me a harness and lower me down."

Of course she was nervous. Of course she was scared. But this was an emergency situation and she could deal with it. A tiny part of her brain objected. She could almost hear her father's condescending tone. But she brushed it away as she stepped into the harness.

"Amber? What do you think you're doing?"

Mud was streaked across Jack's face and clothes.

"My job," she replied as the firefighter clipped on her line.

"Ready?" he asked.

"Ready." She nodded.

Jack's voice cut across everyone's. "No. No way. No way is she going down there. It's too dangerous. Not a chance." His voice was louder than it should be and sent a wave of irritation over her.

She turned toward him. "Stop it, Jack. There are more than enough patients to deal with. Go and look after your own."

His hand came down on her arm in a vise-like grip. "I said no." His voice was steely but it was the expression in his eyes that made her swallow. In a flash she saw a million things she didn't want to. This wasn't the man she'd laughed and loved with last night. This was a man who thought he should be in charge. This was a man who didn't believe in her as a doctor. He didn't respect her as a person and he didn't respect her as a doctor.

She turned to face the firefighter. "Tell him to get his hand off me." Her voice was shaking with rage. A few of the firefighters around them instantly stood up.

"Cool it, buddy."

"You heard the lady. Step back."

Jack's eyes flashed furiously but Amber just jerked her arm away then tugged at her harness to ensure it was secure. She grabbed a few things from her pack and stepped to the opening. "I'm ready." Her heart was thudding frantically in her chest. She felt anything but ready. But delaying now could make things more dangerous for everyone.

"This isn't finished," said Jack hoarsely.

"Oh, yes, it is," she replied as she was lowered down into the darkness.

He could barely contain his rage but he understood exactly how he'd come across. There were four pairs of eyes currently watching him with suspicion. "She's a great doctor. But she's not an emergency doctor. She's never worked in a situation like this."

One of the firefighters met his gaze. "Neither have I. Doesn't mean I won't do the job."

The words almost stung. The guy had a point.

But had that guy lost a woman before that he'd loved? Jack should be down there. Jack should be the one in the position of risk. It shouldn't be Amber. She hadn't asked to be here. She'd just volunteered her services. He didn't doubt she could deal with whatever she might find down there—he didn't doubt her medical abilities at all. What he did doubt was his ability to survive if something were to happen to her.

From the second she'd stepped into that harness, his brain had had to remind himself constantly he wasn't allowed to shout. Because shouting was exactly what he wanted to do right now. Amber didn't need to be at risk. She didn't need to be in a situation that could rapidly go out of control.

He felt himself start to shake. And he couldn't stop it. It was like being dunked in a giant bowl of ice. He wanted to grab that line and haul her back up here. Back up here into his arms where she might actually be safe. Back up here where he could tell her he loved her—despite it only being a week, and despite the fact she still wasn't sure about dating a doctor.

He didn't want to date her. He wanted to marry

her. He wanted to tell her that he could find a job anywhere so long as he was with her. He wanted to tell her that life was too short to wait. That when you knew, you just knew—no matter how hard you tried to fight it.

He lifted his shaking hands to the guys around him. "What can I say? I love her. I don't want anything to happen to her."

There was momentarily a flicker between them all. Then one guy put his hands on Jack's shaking arms. "Then I guess when she gets back up you should tell her."

Jack nodded and took a deep breath. "I guess I should."

She could barely breathe. What should be the inside of a home was a strange hotchpotch like one of those upside-down houses they had at an adventure park. She thought she'd come down the chimney but now she wasn't quite sure. What she was sure of was that the man on the floor beside her was barely alive. She needed oxygen. She needed a chest tube, and any longer and she'd need a defibrillator too. She had to concentrate right now, so why was her head so full of Jack?

She'd been a fool. She'd spent the night with a guy that every warning flag in her brain had told her to stay away from. But she'd done it. She'd let him in. She'd started to believe that all her previous fixed beliefs had been irrational. She shouldn't judge anyone else because of her father. Now the first time she'd opened her heart a little, he'd stamped all over it.

She was more than a fool. She was a stupid fool. And she hated herself more than anything right now. That look he'd given her. As if she were incapable. As if he had a right to tell her what to do.

She couldn't live like that. She *wouldn't* live like that.

There was a loud creak around her and the sound of shifting. A cloud of dust surrounded them and mud was seeping through a gap in the wall near to them—indicating what was waiting. The firefighter on the floor next to her looked up with his eyes wide. "Darn it. We need to move."

The second firefighter who'd come down just behind her was trying to find a way to prop up the huge boulder that had pinned their man to the floor. She finished fastening a collar around her patient's neck. His blood pressure indicated massive internal bleeding. His pulse rate was over one hundred and thirty. She slid her arms under her patient's shoulders. "Okay. Guys, is there any way you can take a bit of the weight even for a few seconds? If you can, I'm going to just yank him out of there."

The two guys nodded and attempted to slide some kind of wedge under the boulder. "You'll have a few seconds. This has an emergency inflatable action. But it won't hold—not with this weight. We'll fire it on three and try and take some of the weight too. Are you ready?"

Amber looked at the strange wedge-shaped contraption that after much manipulation was barely shoved under the huge boulder. Of course it wouldn't hold but it might give her a few seconds. She pressed down low to the floor behind her patient. All she had to do was pull. "Okay."

"One, two, three, *go!*"

She pulled with all her might. There was a tiny explosion followed by a colossal boom. She landed backward on the floor with the patient's head and shoulders planted between her legs. The two firefighters were covered in gray dust and choking madly. The boulder was back squarely on the floor where her patient had just lain.

The creaking sounded again and both guys exchanged a glance. "Let's get him into the cage." Amber didn't have time to recheck his obs as they bundled him into the cage and yanked the cord sharply to get him pulled up. She could hear frantic voices above her as the patient blocked their little light as he was pulled up. Seconds later three lines were dropped down. She didn't even have time to think as one of the firefighters clipped her harness instantly, then yanked her line.

She jerked roughly upward through the thin gap above, banging her shoulder. Arms grabbed her and threw her to one side. The noise was massive. Like a roaring in her ear. She didn't even have time to make sense of any of it. She saw the flash of orange and yellow as the firefighters were pulled up alongside her. "Take cover!" came the shout.

She still hadn't caught her breath when Jack

landed on her, covering her body with his. He had his jacket pulled over his head, which in turn covered hers. Seconds later the ground moved beneath them, then over them, tumbling and tumbling around. Rocks pounded her body. Trees scratched her face and legs. Dirt crowded around her, and when she tried to inhale, mud slid over her mouth, choking her completely. Over and over they went like tumbleweed on a desert landscape. Jack's arms were around her, holding her in place. Nausea washed over her. Her head was spinning.

Finally, the tumbling seemed to slow. She was able to snatch a breath along with a mouthful of leaves. Every part of her ached. She tried to pull her hands up to protect her head, clawing at the jacket that had partially protected her. Jack's.

They finally stopped moving. She wheezed, then choked, spluttering up mouthfuls of dirt and mud. As she turned onto her hands and knees, there was a wave of pain from her ankle. But breathing came first. There was a heavy weight on her back. She pushed up, struggling to move. She tried again, ignoring all her pain and putting all her energy into curling her back around. Dirt and earth moved around her. She coughed, as she burst up through the mounds of debris. Her breathing was stuttered, her head still swimming.

Another landslide. They'd been caught in another landslide. She looked around, trying to work out where she was. Trying to work out where *anyone* was.

At the top right of her vision she could see the flicker of dark green tarpaulin. The triage tent. It seemed a million miles away now.

She shook her head, pulling twigs and leaves from her hair. She blinked. Something warm was beneath her palm.

She looked down, her eyes taking a few seconds to focus.

Jack. It was Jack.

She shifted her hand. "Jack? Are you okay?"

He'd dived on her. He must have realized the landslide had started. He must have known she was about to be caught in it.

Why hadn't he moved away? Why hadn't he got to safety?

She blinked again. He hadn't moved. More important, his chest wasn't moving. His lips were distinctly blue.

She felt a wave of panic. He'd tried to save her. He'd tried to shield her from the landslide. He'd put himself in harm's way deliberately for her. But at what cost?

"Jack! Jack!" She started thudding down on his chest. Trying desperately for any kind of reaction.

Nothing. Nothing at all. She thrust her fingers in at his neck, trying to locate a pulse. Nothing. She moved them again. Still nothing.

Panic gripped her. No. Not Jack. Not now.

"Help!" she shouted, waving one hand frantically in the air. "I need help!"

She started doing chest compressions, letting her doctor mode send her into automatic pilot while every other part of her being screamed out loud.

She loved him. She hated him. She couldn't possibly be with him. But did she really want to live without him when he'd connected with her in ways she'd never felt before?

The pain in her chest was immense. Stress, fear and terror all at once.

She could feel the movement of his chest beneath her palms. His color hadn't improved. He wasn't breathing. She couldn't feel the beat of a heart beneath her hands.

A tear dripped down her cheek and landed onto his chest.

This couldn't be how this ended. It just couldn't be.

She wouldn't let it.

She *couldn't* let it.

CHAPTER TEN

ONE SECOND HE was trying to contain himself; next second he was watching the mass of boulders and tree slide toward them as he dived on top of Amber.

He couldn't remember anything after that.

Except that his chest hurt. *A lot.*

And so did his shoulder. And so did his head.

He blinked, then squinted at the bright white that met his eyes.

A face appeared above him. "Oh, you're back to the land of the living. About time. I know someone that will be pleased."

His brain was still trying to focus. She was vaguely familiar. "Please don't make me do neuro obs on you, Jack. You haven't exactly been the easiest patient these past few hours."

She winked at him and something flooded into his brain. "Lana?" The ER nurse who had been sent out with him and Amber.

Amber. This wasn't a flood; this was a tidal wave. "Amber? Where's Amber?" He tried to sit up in the bed, yelping as his shoulder let him know who was in charge.

Lana smiled. "Oh, good. No neuro obs. You do know who we are." She pointed to his shoulder. "You dislocated that. It will probably be sore for a few days. And you've got a few cracked ribs where someone got a little overenthusiastic when you needed CPR."

"What?" He sagged back on the bed and put his hand on his chest. That was why it was so sore.

"As for Amber." Lana nodded over her shoulder. "Don't let it be said we're not accommodating. She's just back from Theater. Her ankle needed to be pinned. She's just about ready to wake up."

Jack turned his head to the side. There, in the bed next to him, lay a very pale-faced Amber, her dark hair fanned around her, doing her best impersonation of Snow White.

He shook his head, but, no, even that hurt. Lana walked over and lifted a cup with a drinking straw. "Try some water. Then we can chat. Do you need some more analgesia?"

He shook his head. "What…what happened? Last thing I remember was the landslide."

Lana nodded. "I think I'll leave Amber to discuss that with you. She used a few choice words." Lana laughed; her eyes were twinkling. "Give me five minutes to wake her up."

Lana pressed a button and the top of Jack's bed rose behind him, giving him a better view of the room. From the noise outside, the hospital was still crazy. He should be helping. He shouldn't be in here as a patient.

But he couldn't deny the pain in his chest. His heart gave a leap as he heard a few quiet words from the bed next door. He could hear Lana speaking to Amber. "Yeah, I'm the girl with all the gifts. I've been in the ER, Maternity and Surgical in the last day. I just go wherever I'm needed." Lana glanced over her shoulder and gave Jack a wink. "Here, have a little drink and I'll sit you up. Your partner in crime has woken up too."

"He has?" Jack's breath caught at the tone of her voice. She sounded almost…happy?

Lana stepped back and glanced from one to the other as she placed a buzzer next to Amber's hand. "Okay, people, things to do. Ring if you need me." She was laughing to herself as she walked out of the door.

For a few seconds there was silence. And Jack was glad of it. He was just so glad to see her there. Seeing that giant amount of earth moving toward them had terrified him. There had been no chance to move Amber out of its path. He might have had a chance to run for it. The firefighters next to him had run like lightning, carrying the patient in the rescue litter. He only hoped they'd managed to get out of the way of the landslide.

"You made it," he finally said, his voice breaking a little.

"Of course I made it," she snapped. "I haven't finished being mad at you yet."

He rested his head back against the pillow, closed his eyes and smiled. Just the way he liked her.

"What are you smiling at?"

He put his hand to his chest. "I'm just thanking someone up above that we're both still here." He opened his eyes again. She was too far away to reach out to. But that didn't stop him wanting to.

She cleared her throat. "I'm still mad at you."

He met her gaze. Somehow he'd never seen anyone look quite so beautiful. "I get that. Do you think being mad could last a lifetime?"

Confusion swept her face. "What are you talking about?"

He breathed slowly, then winced. He should have remembered about the ribs.

"Are you okay?"

He shook his head. "Just feels like someone has been tap-dancing on my chest. I broke a few ribs, and dislocated a shoulder. I still have no idea how we got out of that."

She blinked. Her eyes looked wet. "Sorry. My technique might be off."

Something clicked in his brain. "You did CPR on me?"

She let out an exasperated laugh. "Well, you'd shielded me from a landslide. It would have seemed kind of bad to leave you there when you—" her voice broke "—you weren't breathing." He saw her try to take a deep breath. "Blue really isn't your color."

His brain was trying to compute. He'd just figured that one of the search and rescue guys or gals had pulled him from the landslide.

She kept talking. "How could I walk away? You tackled me to the ground like you were some kind of superhero. Then you just threw a coat over us and didn't let go all the way down the mountainside."

He wasn't imagining it. A tear was sliding down her cheek.

"Some people are worth holding on to," he said softly.

Amber shook her head. "But we're wrong for each other. You don't believe in me. You second-guess me. You make me feel as if I have to prove myself around you." Her head-shaking got fiercer. "That's not what love is about. That isn't how someone who loves you should make you feel."

He could see it. The pain on her face that had been etched there since he first met her—always just hiding beneath the surface as she slipped on her bravado and her game face.

"Is that how I make you feel, or is that how you already feel, Amber?" he probed gently. "Because I think you're a wonderful doctor. I've seen you in situations that should be completely out of your comfort zone and taking it in your stride. Am I a control freak? Yes. I've lived the past eight years in a place where discipline and control is everything. But where acting first is sometimes the only chance you get. I know that. I recognize that.

"I've had a situation where everything was out of my control and I woke up the next day having lost someone that I loved. How do you think I felt when I saw you put yourself in danger? Did I overreact? Probably, yes. Will I do it in future? Maybe. It doesn't make me a bad person. It makes me know that I feel again. That I love again. Do you think I could bear waiting to see if something might happen to you? I saw that ground start to move, felt the rumble beneath my feet, and there was no way I was letting go of you." He could feel his hands start to shake again. It was almost as if all his emotions were finally coming to the surface.

"Love isn't perfect, Amber. I don't even know if I'm any good at it. I just know I want to try. And I want to try with you. I know we're right at the beginning. I know anything can happen from here. I just want you to give me a chance. I just want to try."

"You love me?" She said the words in disbelief.

"Of course I love you. What's not to love? You fight with me. You tell me I snore. You tease me. You make me work harder. You challenge me at every turn." He gave her a smile. "I don't think I've ever met anyone so perfect for me in my life."

Tears were tumbling down her cheeks. "But… but…"

"But what?"

He fumbled around the edge of the bed until he found the button that lowered the side. He swung his legs to the edge of the bed and waited a few seconds while his head spun, then yanked the blood-pressure cuff from his arm.

The first step was shaky. The second was determined. Nothing would keep him from being by her side. He reached the edge of her bed.

"Tell me how you feel, Amber. Tell me how you feel about me. I might be completely crazy here." He lifted his hand to the bandage on his head. "Maybe I've got a head injury." Then he took his hand back down to his chest. "Or maybe I'm finally listening to my heart." He reached over and brushed one of the tears away from her cheek. "I've spent the last two years focused on work. Locking myself away from everything and everybody." He held up his hands and smiled. "Here. This place." He laughed and shook his head, ignoring the pain. "We came here expecting a busman's holiday. Expecting the beauty and wonder of Hawaii. Instead we got this. A hurricane. Chaos. A landslide." He moved closer and took one of her hands in his. "I'm glad, Amber. I'm glad. Because something brought us together. And whatever you want to do in the future, wherever you want to be—" he smiled at her "—I'm just praying you'll let me tag along."

He moved his other hand over hers too. "I'm not your father, Amber. I'm not your ex. I'll never be those people. I'm Jack Campbell from a tiny mining village in Scotland. Auchinleck. I'll teach you how to say it. I'll take you there. I can promise I'll introduce you to things you've never seen before." As his mind filled with the thoughts of his village back home and the characters it was filled with, he couldn't help but laugh out loud. "They'll love you. Just like I do."

Amber's tears were flowing; she started to laugh. "I wanted to shout at you. I've wanted you to wake up so I could tell you how mad I was at you."

He leaned one arm on the side of her bed. "And what exactly were you mad about, Dr. Berkeley?"

It seemed as though all her emotions welled up at once. "I... I was mad because you put yourself at risk to try and save me." She was struggling to get the words out. "I was mad because you were trying to stop me doing something dangerous... I was mad because I was scared to do it...but I didn't want to be. I was mad because I constantly felt as if I had to prove myself to my father. To earn his respect. To earn his approval. To show him I could do it. To show him I was capable. And... I... I..." She stopped talking and sucked in a deep breath. Her tear-filled eyes met his. It was almost as if something had just clicked into place. He could see the glimmer of recognition in her gaze. She squeezed his hand. "And... I don't need to do that with you."

He could see her whole change in stance. Her shoulders went down as if the tension had left her body. "I don't need to do that with you," she repeated in a whisper.

"No." He smiled. "You don't, Amber. I've got your back. I'll always have your back. You specialize in infectious diseases. How much of that have you got to do in the last seven days? Have you complained? Have you said no? Not once. You've put your head down and got on with it. And have you stopped when you were scared? When you put yourself in a situation where you could be electrocuted? When you put yourself in the path of the landslide?" He cupped her cheek. "Who would do that, Amber?" Then he laughed again. "What normal, sane-minded person would do a thing like that?"

She started laughing too. "Jack Campbell, I do believe you may be a bad influence on me."

He fumbled around, looking for her button to lower the bedside. "Where is this dang thing? Ah…finally." He put the side down and moved closer, wincing as his ribs let him know he wasn't quite as healed as he might want to be.

He put one hand on his side. "Dr. Berkeley, I believe we may need to talk about your technique."

"Hang the technique." She smiled as she put her hand around his head and pulled him closer. "You're alive, aren't you?"

He moved closer, inches away from her lips. "I believe that might put me in your debt."

She licked her lips. "You bet it does. You don't think I saved the man I love for anyone else, do you?"

Before he could ask her to repeat that, she kissed him.

And he had absolutely no intention of stopping that…

EPILOGUE

One year later

EVERYTHING WAS PERFECT. The beach was perfect. The brightly colored flowers in her wedding bouquet were perfect, and the overwater bungalows in the perfect green sea in front of them were perfect—especially when she knew one of them had their names on it.

"Ready?"

Her mother stood in front of her dressed in a bright orange dress, complete with an over-the-top hat on her head. So right for the mother of the bride.

Amber stared down and wiggled her pink-painted toenails in the yellow sand. They were always going to come back to the place they'd met to cement their union. Hawaii had recovered well and returned to the beautiful lush state it had been on the morning she'd first arrived.

She ran her hand across her pale cream wedding dress. She'd opted for a three-quarter-length dress, lightweight, with lace across her décolletage and shoulders with cap sleeves. Covered enough for a bride but quirky enough that she could get away with being barefoot. Her only jewelry was her gold locket.

She nodded and breathed slowly. "Oh, yes. I'm ready."

Her mother stepped in front of her and put a hand on each shoulder. "I always wondered if I'd have to tell my daughter not to make the same mistakes I did. You have no idea how happy I am that I don't need to do it. I love Jack. He's perfect for you. Grumpy sometimes. Doesn't let you get away with anything. But most importantly he adores you, Amber. I see it in his eyes every time he looks at you. Work hard at this marriage, honey. You found a keeper."

Tears threatened to spill down her cheeks. She leaned forward and hugged her mom, almost sending the bright orange hat tumbling down the beach in the light winds. "Thank you, Mom, for everything. You've always been my biggest supporter and I love you."

"Come on, Amber! Are you stalling, girl?"

The broad Scots voice of Jack's dad drifted down the beach. His family were waiting in the shaded area, tugging at the collars of their shirts in the searing heat. They'd been ecstatic to come to Hawaii for the wedding, even though it was a long flight. It was a small wedding with only a few other members of Amber's family, and a few of the residents they'd met in Hawaii. Lana, Jamal and Ron were all waiting patiently for things to start, as were Aaron and Zane—who'd both made a good recovery from meningitis—both with their respective parents.

Amber laughed and turned around, catching her breath at the sight of Jack waiting for her in his kilt. "Oh, wow."

Her mother gave her hand a squeeze. "Yip. Wow. Let's not keep your handsome man waiting. These Scots guys can't seem to manage the heat," she joked.

Amber met Jack's gaze. She'd never been so sure of anything in her life.

He gave her his trademark cheeky grin. His heavy dark kilt was swaying in the breeze from the ocean and his cream open-necked ghillie shirt outlined his muscled chest. As she walked toward him, he held out his hand to her.

She handed her flowers to her mother and he took both her hands in his so they were facing each other.

"You've still got a few seconds," he whispered. "If you want to do the runaway bride, you should do it now."

She smiled at the celebrant who was waiting to start the ceremony as she let go of Jack's hands, slid her hands around his neck and stepped closer.

"Where would I run to? I'm exactly where I want to be, with exactly who I want to be with. Now and always."

The celebrant gave a short laugh. "Hey, folks. Aren't you supposed to wait for me?"

Jack winked. "Just give us a minute. We'll be right with you," he said as he bent to kiss his bride.

And the guests all applauded, even though they weren't quite husband and wife.

And everything was just as it was destined to be.

* * * * *